A Mystery at Moor House

Lady Ellen Investigates

Kelly Mason

LITTLE ORCHARD PRESS

Editor: Becky Halls

Cover design by: www.getcovers.co.uk

This book was written in the UK and edited in British English, where some spelling, grammar and word usage will be different to US English.

For Tammy

Chapter One

My hair blew in the summer breeze as I meandered through the Somerset countryside in my blue Rolls-Royce, with the roof down. It had been delivered to The Grand Hotel in Branden Bay where I had been staying. One of the men who had spent time recovering at my once-busy convalescent home had sold it to me. It had cost rather a lot but – as I drove along the lanes with my companion Lottie and my dog Prince beside me, with his ears flapping behind him – it felt well worth it.

"This is so much fun, Ellen," Lottie called to me as she held onto her hat. "Even if I'm getting squashed by Prince."

I laughed. "We'll be there soon," I said. "If I put him in the back I'm worried he'll jump out when we reach a junction."

We were off to spend two weeks with a dear friend of mine, Lady Phoebe Denham. She was my life-long best friend, whom I'd grown up with at the boarding school in Gloucestershire we had both attended. Our destinies had taken different turns since we'd left school. Phoebe had soon fallen in love during her first season and had been married to the Earl of Denham within months, a pairing approved by both sets of parents. She was mother to twin girls. Whereas I'd married an untitled man, Leonard Tamar, before inheriting Ashcombe Hall and estate from my dear papa who was taken from me following a short but devastating illness. I was only married a few short months before I lost my beloved Leo. I'd thrown myself into the war effort, turning my ancestral home into a place where injured men could convalesce. The hall had remained open to the injured long after the war concluded, having taken men from other homes as they closed. The hall was now free of patients and undergoing refurbishment to return it to the way I remembered it as a child.

"How far away are we?" Lottie called out.

"Not far," I said as I turned a corner. "Maybe a mile?"

I had met Lottie Penny whilst staying at Millar's Hotel in the seaside resort of Branden Bay. I had taken her under my wing, employing her as my assistant.

However, over the weeks we had spent together, I had come to regard her more as the younger sister I never had. She was ten years my junior and had a zest for life which cheered me.

"What's Lady Denham like?" Lottie asked.

"Phoebe and I went to school together and had such fun. Getting up to all sorts of mischief and staying up at night gossiping with our other friend Jane. Looking back, I feel we were a bit of a handful for the teachers." Our mutual friend Jane was also married, and lived on Ashcombe's neighbouring estate. Although we did not have such a fond attachment these days. I rather felt that she and her husband did not approve of me. I often found that certain members of the aristocracy preferred to keep things traditional and were not as eager as I was to move with the times.

"Boarding school sounds great. Sebastian loved his," Lottie said. "I wish he would write to me." She looked away at the scenery. "I've not heard from him for weeks. I hope he's alright."

Sebastian, also known as the Earl of Garthorn, was the son of the Marquis of Bandberry. Lottie had worked for The Bandberrys in their Mayfair house whilst in service. However, it was my opinion that the relationship was destined for heartbreak. Upon learning of their son's affection for Lottie, his family had banished her to the other side of the country. I was now carrying a burden of knowledge. Before leaving Branden Bay, I had read a newspaper report that Sebastian's parents had announced his engagement to a titled young lady in Ireland. I had yet to divulge this information to Lottie as I assumed the young man would write to her and explain himself. I had asked the hotel to forward any post they received for us to Denham Hall. But if Lottie did not hear from him, I knew I would have to tell her myself, before she suffered the embarrassment of discovering the truth from a third party.

"I'm sure you'll hear from him soon," I said as I turned into the long hedge lined drive.

Prince barked as Denham Hall loomed up before us.

"This is massive," Lottie said. She had yet to see my own residence, Ashcombe Hall, which was in fact twice the size of Denham.

As I stopped the motorcar, a footman approached us.

"Welcome to Denham Hall, Lady Ellen and Miss Penny."

"It's been too long, Elks," I said as I got out of the car. "Come along, Prince."

My Irish setter jumped from Lottie's lap. He had a glossy red coat and short legs with slightly wonky eyes, having been the runt of his litter. But Prince had grown into a strong and faithful dog.

"Ellen!" Phoebe approached me across the gravel. She wore a modern dress in a pale green, with a drop waist. She too had bobbed hair. It had been years since we had seen each other. Back then, we both had long hair pinned up.

She greeted me with an embrace. "I'm quite overcome now we're together." She wiped a tear from her eye. "I'm so pleased to see you."

It was in that moment that I realised how I had neglected myself and our friendship, in my quest to try and make the world a better place. A world that had dealt me a great blow.

Phoebe turned to Lottie. "And this must be Charlotte."

"Pleased to meet you, Lady Denham." Lottie curtsied.

Phoebe smiled at her. "I'm so excited to hear all about the adventures you two have been having. I'm quite jealous."

"I'd love to hear your stories as well, Lady Denham," Lottie said. "About your school days."

Phoebe laughed. "You'll probably soon tire of those as I intend to reminisce with Ellen at every available opportunity." She threaded her arm into mine. "Now, do come along. I have luncheon set on the lawn. It's such a glorious day."

We followed her through the house as Lottie looked about in awe. The walls were adorned with portraits of earls and their families. We found ourselves in the garden, having passed through large French doors onto a patio. A huge croquet lawn was set on the left and beyond that, luncheon had been spread on a table underneath a large oak tree.

"This is so beautiful, my lady," Lottie said to Phoebe.

"I love my home," Phoebe said. "Denham Hall is at its best during the summer months."

We enjoyed cucumber sandwiches and fancy cakes whilst Lottie and I told Phoebe all about the two cases we had solved in Branden Bay.

"You've always had a strong sense of right and wrong," Phoebe said to me. "I think it suits you."

"Remember how the headmistress used to scold us for being nosey?" I said with a laugh.

Phoebe giggled. "Especially when we caught her with the caretaker."

I gasped. "I had quite forgotten that!"

"Next you will be opening a detective agency," Phoebe said to me with a laugh. "And tell me more about this Captain Hamilton, he sounds divine!"

"He's a very handsome man," Lottie said. "And he adores Ellen.'

"Of course he doesn't," I said, reaching for my fan.

"I have the impression that you're rather fond of him," Phoebe said. "Your eyes light up every time you mention his name. I may not have seen you for years but I can tell when you like a fellow."

"Nonsense," I said, but I knew deep down I liked Hamilton very much indeed.

"It wouldn't hurt to be a bit more carefree," Phoebe said. "I've been worried about you, keeping your distance and focusing on the hall for so many years."

She had a point and I was surprised at how I was fighting against accepting it. Although I was sitting with my best friend Phoebe and Lottie the young woman I now saw as a younger sister, I did not feel ready to let my guard down and acknowledge any feelings towards Hamilton. I had the future of Ashcombe Hall to think of and did not have time to entertain romance.

"I'm glad we're here," I said, changing the subject. "I'm looking forward to a couple of weeks relaxation before returning to Branden Bay. And then we will return to Ashcombe in September."

Lottie beamed at me. "I'm so lucky that Ellen has employed me as her assistant."

"Lottie, you will love Ashcombe," Phoebe said.

"I'm looking forward to seeing Sebastian again." She sighed.

I caught Phoebe's gaze. Sebastian had of course come up in conversation when we were discussing our last case with Phoebe. I had written ahead to Phoebe and advised her of the delicate situation and that I had yet to break the news to Lottie that her childhood sweetheart was now betrothed to another.

Prince bounded up and dropped a stick at Lottie's feet. She threw the stick for him and then followed.

"She's such a delightful young woman," Phoebe said.

"I feel very protective of her," I said.

"When are you going to break the news about Lord Garthorn's engagement?" Phoebe whispered, in case her voice was to travel on the breeze.

"I was rather hoping the young man would have written. But he has not and I cannot run the risk of Lottie finding out in any other fashion, so have decided to tell her tomorrow, after the post has been delivered, if communication has not arrived."

"The poor thing," Phoebe said. "Although I would not want Lady Bandberry to be my mother-in-law."

"Her banishment offer to Lottie was schooling in Switzerland." I shook my head. "Lottie turned down the opportunity of a lifetime." She stroked Prince as he sat beside her.

"And now Sebastian has abandoned her," Phoebe said with a sigh.

"I will do whatever I can to provide her with an excellent education when we return to Ashcombe. She deserves it. I am more than able to fund finishing school in Switzerland if that is her desire."

"You really have taken Lottie into your heart, Ellen, and I think she's good for you." She looked over to Lottie who was now walking towards us. "Although, I wouldn't send her away."

As Lottie approached with a beam on her face, I dreaded the awkward discussion I feared lay ahead of me.

Chapter Two

Four days later, I walked down the winding staircase of Denham Hall from a wonderfully restful night's sleep. I could already hear Phoebe and Lottie's voices floating from the breakfast room. Once inside, I took a seat beside Lottie but before I could join in with their conversation, the housekeeper entered.

"The post, my lady." Mrs Heath passed me a letter.

"Is it a letter from Sebastian?" Lottie asked as she looked at the envelope in my hand.

Since I had broken the news to her that, according to the newspapers, Sebastian was now betrothed, Lottie had spent two complete days sobbing and wishing to be alone, accompanied by Prince who had whined, not leaving her side. By the third day, she was convinced it was a mix-up and that

Sebastian would never agree to marry the young woman, Lady Clara. Lottie spoke of nothing else other than the love she shared with him. Although, with her keeping to her room for a couple of days, it had been an ideal opportunity for me to catch up with Phoebe. Her husband Henry, the Earl of Denham, was away on business so we indulged in much gossip. Even though Phoebe spent most of her time at Denham Hall with her daughters, she still seemed to know an awful lot of what was occurring in society, especially since she had acquired a telephone.

"Will you stare at the letter for much longer?" Phoebe asked, bringing me out of my daydream.

I looked at the envelope in my hand and my heart gave a flutter, for I knew it was not from Sebastian, but from Hamilton. I recognised his handwriting and resisted the temptation to lift the envelope to my face, to check whether there was any trace of his cologne.

"It's from Captain Hamilton," I said to Lottie.

Her flash of disappointment was nearly imperceptible as she smiled at me. "Maybe he wants to see you?"

I opened the envelope and scanned the letter. She was correct. "Us," I said. "He wants to see us and we're invited to Dulverton for a garden party." I could barely hide the excitement from my voice.

"Ooh, exciting," Phoebe said.

"That's nice," Lottie said. "Are you sure you want me to come?"

"Of course," I said. "He specifically invited you and Prince."

"What does he say?" Phoebe asked as she lifted the cloche from the eggs.

"He gives directions of how to get there, it shouldn't take too long."

"How super, and ideal," Phoebe said. "As I have to go into Exeter with the girls tomorrow, to meet Henry and his friend from University – the Duke of Loxborough. I was going to suggest you accompanied us as he's the most sought after man in the South West, but it appears you already have an attractive offer." She took the letter from me. "Ah, the affection Captain Hamilton holds for you oozes between the lines."

"Nonsense." I paused. "Maybe I should not accept the invitation," I said in a haughty voice.

"Ellen, don't take any notice of our teasing," Lottie said, clearly sensing my embarrassment. "I'm missing the Captain, too. There's no shame in that!"

Prince barked.

I laughed. "It appears all three of us are missing him. And it's too late to send our apologies, as he has made no mention of a telephone. We would arrive before the mail. I would not wish for him to wait and for us not to arrive."

* * *

The following day, first thing, Phoebe had left for Exeter with the children. I did not wish to arrive at the house in Dulverton too early, so took Prince for a walk around the estate in an effort to tire him out. He would hopefully sleep on the back seat of my car, so Lottie would be comfortable, without him lolloping on her lap in the front.

Phoebe's estate was quite beautiful with its hilly terrain, a contrast to the flat land of the Ashcombe estate. The flat land was practical as far as farming was concerned, however I loved Denham Hall with its wooded hills and tufty land, most of it natural and unfarmed. Having walked for some time, I came to Phoebe's walled garden and opened the gate. I stopped and watched as insects and butterflies fluttered in amongst an array of stunning and sweet-smelling blooms, from lavender to roses and exquisite flowers I could not identify, sourced from foreign lands. I breathed in deeply as I walked around, then jumped as a man stood up before me.

"Sorry to startle you, my lady!" He doffed his hat.

I laughed. "Wakeman, it's good to see you after so long."

Prince jumped up at him.

"Hello, boy. I've not seen you since you were a pup. A little scrap you were, too."

I laughed "He's certainly a strong dog now." I gestured around the garden. "Such a beautiful array of plants. You're truly talented."

"I can give you a tour?" He rubbed his grey beard.

I glanced at my wristwatch. "Ah, it will have to wait until tomorrow, I'm afraid. I'm leaving within the hour for a garden party in Dulverton."

"Today? I'd stay inside if I were you!" he said with a frown.

"Whatever for?" I asked.

"The rains." He looked at the sky.

I raised my gaze spotting only a few wisps of white cloud. "It's a clear day."

He shook his head. "I smells it in the air. Storm's a coming, mark my words."

"Hopefully it'll arrive after the garden party," I said. "I'll be sure not to stay too late."

He sighed. "I'd take heed. I told Lady Denham to be back before the strike of three."

I considered Wakeman was being somewhat melodramatic. "Thank you for the warning," I said, then bade him farewell and took Prince back to the house.

As I entered the French doors, Lottie approached me.

"What shall we take with us?" she asked.

"I imagine we'll only stay for a few hours," I said. "However, if they do invite us to stay for supper, we may wish to change our clothes." Wakeman's warning repeated in my head. "And if the weather turns, we may wish also to have warmer attire. The gardener spoke of a storm later."

Lottie frowned. "But it's sunny outside."

"Better to be safe than sorry. We can put the trunk in the back of the motorcar with a complete change of clothes for both of us. I'll also bring a supply of food for Prince. We can't expect them to cater for him. I'll keep the roof in place for the journey, it will be easier to manage him."

I was pleased I had brought my motorcar. Dulverton did not have rail links and Moor House was on the outskirts of the small market town, on the edge of Exmoor surrounded by woodland. Hamilton had described it to me in his letter and it sounded beautiful.

Once we had loaded the motorcar with the help of Phoebe's footman, we left the Denham Estate. There was not a cloud in the sky and I was sure Wakeman had been mistaken.

As we reached Dulverton, we took the stone bridge over the River Barle.

"It's lovely here," Lottie said as we travelled through the town on our way to the house, using the instructions Hamilton had provided in his letter. We drove along a lane running parallel to the babbling river and soon reached a narrow wooden bridge which I took slowly. I held my breath and prayed it would take the weight of the motorcar. It creaked as we crossed and I breathed a sigh of relief once we reached the other side.

After a short incline, we came upon the sign which informed us that we had arrived at Moor House. We turned into the small drive, which lead downwards though a hydrangea lined drive towards the pretty residence. I stopped the engine and took it all in. It was not grand like my home or the hall at Denham. It was a sprawling stonebuilt Victorian-style large family house.

As I continued down the drive, I spotted Hamilton striding towards us with the walking stick he always carried. I gulped, feeling momentarily bashful. He looked extremely handsome. His face was tanned, I presumed from being outside during the warm weather. He was employed at the property on a short contract, ensuring there was decent security in place as there had been a number of thefts in the local area.

Lottie waved at him. "Hi, Captain."

"Hello, I'm so pleased you came." Hamilton opened the motorcar door for me. He took my hand and helped me out. I stood for a moment, gazing into his eyes and debating whether or not I should kiss him on the cheek. That was what I wanted to do but, up until that time, we had not shown each other that level of affection.

Lottie exited the car from the other side and ran around to Hamilton, grinning before throwing her arms around him. I took a step backwards and smiled. She displayed her emotions with such ease. Prince jumped from the car and I caught his leash to prevent him launching himself at Hamilton.

"I missed you, Captain," Lottie said, grinning up at him.

"Let's not be so formal out here," he said. "Please, call me Ernest."

Lottie beamed. "Of course, Ernest." She released him and then grabbed Prince's leash from me. "I'll take this one for a comfort break."

I felt a little nervous as she hurried away, pulling Prince with her. He appeared to want to return and jump up at Hamilton. I smiled as I wracked my brain for something to say. Then I remembered the delicate situation regarding Sebastian.

Once Lottie was out of earshot I turned to Hamilton. "I'm not sure whether you read in the newspaper..."

"About Sebastian? Yes," he said. "I find it hard to believe. It would not surprise me if his parents announced the engagement without even consulting the young man."

"The family wish the pair to be wed and it appears that is why he was taken to Ireland. Lottie told me that he had not seen the young woman, Lady Clara, since he was eleven years old."

"Surely Sebastian would not agree to marry a woman he does not know?"

"You would not think so, but curiously, Lottie has yet to hear from him, which is odd considering he used to write her every day. He may feel duty-bound to comply with his family's wishes."

"How is the poor girl taking it?" Hamilton asked.

"We've discussed it at length," I said. "Lottie is refusing to accept Sebastian has asked for Lady Clara's hand in marriage until she has heard directly from him."

"Lottie deserves to be happy but, as we have discussed before, it is an unlikely pairing." Hamilton sighed. "And from the photograph in the newspaper, Lady Clara would appear to be a handsome young woman and of Sebastian's own class."

I shook my head. "I should never have encouraged the relationship between them."

"Don't blame yourself, Ellen. I was also taken by the affection they displayed. Now, let me show you around the garden before the rain comes in."

"Rain?" I said.

He offered me his arm. "Apparently so. We're expecting a shower."

As I looked up, I saw clouds approaching. *Maybe Wakeman was right?* I thought.

"And then I will introduce you to our host, Conrad Doyle," Hamilton said.

We walked around the side of the house until we reached the gardens. They consisted of a flat and well maintained lawn, which could easily be used for croquet, surrounded by a gravel path from which sprawling lawns, dotted with manicured bushes and small trees, sloped towards a dark woodland.

"It's idyllic," I said.

"Lady Ellen."

I swung around to find a man I would say to be in his mid-forties standing before me, outstretching his arm. Hamilton released my arm and I took Conrad's hand. He was attractive with salt and pepper slicked back hair. From his accent, I could tell he came from a northern part of England.

He lifted my hand and kissed it. "Charmed," he said as I was dealt a waft of his heady cologne. "I'm Conrad Doyle and I'm so pleased you accepted my invitation, my lady."

"Thank you, Mr Doyle." I smiled at him and tried not to sneeze, wondering whether he had bathed in the cologne, it was so strong.

"Please, call me Conrad." He smiled at me. "I understand you assisted Captain Hamilton with his investigations in Branden Bay."

I looked to Hamilton and frowned. I was hardly a top detective and felt I had stumbled around the investigations, but I was a lot more significant than Hamilton's assistant.

Hamilton turned to face Conrad. "It was Lady Ellen who sought to investigate, I merely helped her. As I've already explained." Hamilton had a frown upon his face. I sensed that Mr Doyle was a man to grate upon his nerves.

"I admire an intelligent woman." Mr Doyle offered his arm to me. "Shall we have a look around the gardens before the rain falls?" He looked up at the sky. "We're having drinks on the lawn but luncheon will be served inside."

I let the man lead me away, since he was my host, but threw a wistful glance to Hamilton, who was left standing alone.

"Hamilton," Conrad called over his shoulder. "Do another turn of the periphery, to make sure all entry points are secure."

Hamilton hesitated, then replied: "Of course, Mr Doyle."

"That should take him at least half an hour," Conrad said with a chuckle as Hamilton walked away.

"It'll give us time to become better acquainted. I'm so pleased you came." He led me away. "Hamilton's a good chap, met him in Bristol a few months back."

This trip was not what I was expecting. I was rather hoping to enjoy the party as Hamilton's guest. But it appeared he was working. I felt glum. Conrad had commented that I had accepted *his* invitation. I had thought it was Hamilton who had requested my presence. I took a deep breath, wishing I'd remained at Denham Hall.

Chapter Three

Prince bounded around the garden with his ears flapping. I smiled as Lottie ran after him, one hand holding onto the hat she wore and the other clutching the leash which Prince appeared to have escaped from. He'd learned to wriggle out of it and I needed to purchase a new leash as soon as we returned to Branden Bay. It would not do for him to get loose in a crowd.

"Is that your hound?" Conrad asked, gesturing at my dog.

"He's an Irish setter," I said.

"Bit short for a setter, isn't he?"

"He was the runt. I rescued him moments before my game keeper intended to shoot him."

Conrad stopped in his tracks and gazed into my eyes. "You've such a kind heart, my lady. I heard you rescued men during the war and that many have remained on your land – and that you have a thriving estate."

"I'm lucky they found their way to me," I said. It was true: in a time when many established families were struggling, I was doing rather well. "Ashcombe is self-sufficient. I've been extremely lucky to have experienced farmers on my land as well as tenants. And they've such ingenious ideas. After facing the possibility of death, many men experience a new lease of life."

"You clearly have an astute business mind," Conrad said. "And have been able to move with the times. Some of the big families are so stuck in the old days, they're all spent out."

"It's been a difficult time for many of us," I said with a sigh. But I understood what Conrad was referring to. Families who relied on their investments to support their estates and lifestyle had found themselves unable to deal with any shock events, such as death, tax duties and the changing financial markets.

We resumed our walk and Conrad led me down the slope of the lawn. "I was originally an artist living in the northern counties. I moved south where most of my commissions were. But I've had to diversify to make ends meet. And since then, I've built a thriving art dealing business. Interrupted for some time of course when war broke out. I'm keeping it quiet locally, but I'm holding a silent auction here. I'll have a few interested parties visiting over the coming weekend and am holding this garden party to relax with family a few days before the visitors arrive. The first will be here on Friday."

"The market must be good for you," I said. "I hear many families are selling their heirlooms."

"Indeed, not everyone has been as fortunate as your good self, my lady. But I gather it's your kindness of heart, and your charitable nature, which led to your faithful workforce."

I wondered where Conrad had been hearing so much about me, then of course realised it would have come from Hamilton, who must have been singing my praises. I felt warmed by that thought.

"The art market has become somewhat flooded," Conrad said. "Therefore I'm moving with the tide of fashion into the realms of Egyptian artefacts."

"Really? I've followed with much interest the discovery of the pharaohs' tombs," I said. They had been widely covered in the newspapers and the inner chamber of the most famous tomb had been opened earlier that year. "It's most fascinating," I added.

"It's a booming market, my lady."

"Is it an Egyptian artefact that you're selling here?"

"It is indeed, but I've not told anyone locally. I don't want to attract any thieves."

"Of course not," I said, realising that was why Hamilton had been employed on a short contract.

Ahead of us was a table set out with a teapot and cups, underneath a tree where a young woman sat. She had long hair and gave me a thorough up-and-down look as we approached. She sat back further in her seat as if to gain a better view of me. Her eyes met mine, but she made no effort to stand.

She lit a cigar, exhaled the smoke and smiled. "The famous Lady Ellen of Ashcombe Hall. We've heard so much about you at dinner from Ernie."

I noted that she was using an extremely familiar term for Captain Hamilton. Indeed, I had never heard him being referred to as *Ernie*. I felt my lips purse and then relaxed. I was, after all, in a middle-class residence and not a stately home with titled residents. The manner was bound to be more informal. I gave myself a thorough ticking off for being so snooty.

"This is my daughter, Freddie Doyle," Conrad said.

"I'm pleased to meet you," I said and outstretched my hand.

Freddie lifted her cigar to her mouth, inhaled and slowly let the smoke escape her mouth as I watched, at a loss to how I should react. I simply let my arm return to my side.

Then she spoke: "Ernie entertained us with stories of your investigations." She rolled her eyes. "Father was desperate to meet you. And seeing you in the flesh, it's true you are most beautiful ...for an older woman."

I gave a short laugh to mask my embarrassment. Indeed, I was senior to Freddie Doyle, who I assumed was in her early twenties, but I was not yet thirty. *Do I really look old?* I thought. I was also rather embarrassed that my appearance had been a subject for discussion at the Doyle dining table.

"Please keep your manners in check, Freddie," Conrad said to his daughter, and then turned to me. "It's true. I am an admirer of yours."

"What luck that there's nothing between you and Ernie." Freddie took another puff and then blew out. "He made that quite clear when I quizzed him." She both pouted and smiled at the same time, avoiding my gaze.

I bit my lip, feeling as if someone had punched me. But of course, Hamilton and I had not recently discussed romance, regardless of the fact that we had spent so much time together. Before he left Branden Bay, we had taken many walks along the beach and shared a few meals for two at the local restaurants. It may well have felt like courting, but clearly it was not.

"I'm most honoured to have you here today," Conrad said, filling the awkward silence.

"Calm down Father, let her settle in," Freddie said, then turned to me. "Don't mind him, he's looking for a new wife."

"Freddie," Conrad said in a warning tone.

I felt a complete fool. It was crystal clear that Conrad had invited me as a potential romantic interest, having heard all about the poor widowed Lady Ellen of Ashcombe Hall from his security man. I swallowed away my disappointment and smiled at him, deciding that once luncheon had concluded, I would return immediately to Denham Hall. I was quite pleased that I was staying with Phoebe as I would have someone to discuss this sorry affair with over a nightcap. Hamilton had made it clear, years before, that a union between us would be inappropriate, since I was from the upper classes and he was a middle class man – the son of an accountant. I should have listened and not invented affections in my mind, which were clearly not reciprocated.

We were interrupted by a man dressed in working clothes who approached us. He was as tall as Conrad and had fair hair with a weathered face, which made it difficult for me to judge his age. However, he had a youthful mannerism about him and I guessed he was closer to Freddie's age than mine. "Mr Doyle, Shaw wishes to see you," he said.

"This is Joseph," Conrad said. "He's the best gardener for miles around. And learned all of his skills from our gardens."

"I'm pleased to meet you, Joseph," I said to the young man and forced a smile.

He nodded. "My lady. I hope you have an enjoyable time at Moor House, it's a slice of heaven here."

"Joseph does well for himself, tending the gardens of Dulverton," Conrad said. "And selling his vegetables at the local market. We're most proud of him." There was clear affection in Conrad's tone. He looked in the direction of the house. "I'd better check on Shaw as requested. I'll return as soon as I can." He left us and walked up the slope towards the house.

Freddie rose from her chair. "I'll show you around." She gestured at Joseph who stared after Conrad. "Please tell your mother we'll take luncheon in half an hour in the dining room."

He nodded at her and strode away.

"I think he earns more than Father does," Freddie said with a grim laugh.

"Does your father not mind him working for others?" I asked.

"Joseph tends our gardens in return for his board

and keep. He lives here with his mother. He's been here since he was four years old."

"I see," I said.

Freddie motioned for me to follow. Her dress reached the floor and I guessed it was a family heirloom. Certainly not in fashion. I remembered my grandmother wearing a similar style. Freddie clearly was a woman who shunned the latest fashion, wearing the emerald dress, underneath which I imagined was a corset, considering the shape of her curves. Not an outfit I would wear in the heat of the summer. Her dark wavy hair hung loose over her shoulders. If it had been red, she would have resembled Botticelli's Venus with her porcelain skin. Her eyes had a defiance in them. This was a woman who clearly was never going to fit the mould. The cigar she left on the wrought iron table was a symbol of that. As she picked up her dress, I noticed she was bare footed.

She called over her shoulder. "We'll go into the wood, before the rain comes. Sorry about father," she said as I caught her up. "He's been hanging off Ernie's every word about you. He's desperate for a wife and also a rich one." She turned and smiled at me. "I can tell you've not an ounce of interest in him, otherwise I would not be so candid."

"I had no idea that I was invited here for that

reason," I remarked in a haughty tone. "I expected a busy party and to blend into the crowd."

"You're the guest of honour," Freddie said. "But don't worry, Father's tied up with selling his Egyptian artefact."

"What sort of artefact is it?" I asked.

"I've absolutely no idea. I'm not one of the few permitted to view it." She sighed. "I guess it's some gruesome object from a pharaoh's tomb." She continued into the wood and ran her hand over the bark of a tree as she passed it. "They should leave the things where they find them. It's akin to digging up the local graveyard and stealing jewellery from the corpses. He should have stuck to paintings."

"Why is he selling it here and not at Sotheby's?" I asked.

"To feel important when the prospective buyers arrive – to create a mystery surrounding the piece, the exclusiveness of the by-invitation-only auction. Father loves a spot of drama. It's the artist in him." She stopped and turned to me. "That's been his downfall. I'll be pleased when the dreadful item is gone from here. Especially with The Magpie around."

"You have a bird problem?" I asked.

"No, it's the name given to a local thief. We've had a spate of robberies around the moors. That's why we need the security."

"Ah yes, I remember Captain Hamilton mentioning it to me a couple of weeks ago," I said, recalling that was the reason he was asked to protect the piece.

"The Magpie usually steals jewellery, hence the nickname. He likes shiny objects. Father does not wish to take any chances as we were the first victim of The Magpie. He stole my mother's jewellery."

"How awful," I said.

Freddie put her hand to an emerald necklace. "I have this, this was hers. I wear it constantly. It's enough. I'm not one for opulent accessories or copious amounts of belongings. But there was a ring..."

"What sort of ring?" I asked.

She sighed. "A sapphire with a setting made up of small stars, inscribed on the inside with the words 'Shine Bright'." She took a deep breath, showing me for the first time she was very human. "It was given to my aunt by her husband. She was involved in the women's movement and died whilst battling for our rights."

"I'm so sorry that something so precious with such meaning was lost. And, of course, for the life of your aunt." As I followed Freddie, I beat down my inquisitive nature. I could not help thinking: *I wonder who this Magpie fellow is?*

Chapter Four

I followed Freddie down a path through the small wood, where exposed roots of trees were covered in bright green moss, looking as if they were draped with an emerald fur. I wondered whether the leafy path felt uncomfortable for Freddie with her bare feet. If it did, she didn't show it.

"I hear water," I said. "I take it the river is nearby?"

"Yes, but we can't walk down to the bank from here, it's too steep." She stopped at a railing with a padlocked gate, pausing as if her mind had clouded over. On the other side of the gate was a large tree with a thick trunk encrusted with moss with branches that stretched out like multiple limbs, I assumed it was hundreds of years old. Freddie looked around as if making sure no one else was there and reached into the top of her dress, removed a key, then opened the padlock. "Follow me, but do be careful not to slip."

I moved cautiously as the forest floor was not flattened there. We sat down on a bench positioned the other side of the tree, looking down the steep slope to the water below. Freddie dusted off her feet. Before her was a collection of relatively fresh flowers laid upon the ground.

"I come here often – to remember," she said.

"Remember?" I asked.

She nodded at the drop to the river. "Mother slipped, she broke her body on the way down."

"How awful," I said.

"She was alive when Ivy, our housekeeper, found her but had passed away by the time Shaw and Joseph managed to get her back up to the house." She paused. "It was a shock."

"I'm so sorry," I said.

"It was a couple of years ago now. I left for London soon after. Life's too short and I didn't want to spend it watching father live his debauched lifestyle. It was disgraceful the way he carried on with no period of mourning whatsoever."

"Shock hits people in different ways," I said gently.

"As soon as the funeral was completed he began the parties. And..." She paused. "If Father had not been in Exeter that day, I would not have put it past him to have pushed Mother himself." She sighed.

Oh dear, I thought, contemplating her shocking opinion.

We sat for a couple of minutes in silence. I listened to the crows chattering over the sound of the rushing water below. I felt so sad that Freddie's mother had died here. I guessed the damp forest floor, sloping with green moss, made it somewhat treacherous.

Freddie changed the subject. "I hope you were not taken with Father. If so, I've dashed your opinion of him."

"I have no interest in romance," I said tactfully because, if I had, Conrad Doyle would not have been on my list.

Freddie glanced over my shoulder. "So, no interest in Ernie?" she asked with a coy smile.

"Absolutely not," I said in a defiant voice which came out much louder than I had anticipated.

She smiled as I heard leaves rustle and turned to see Hamilton staring down at me.

He glanced to the slope. "I understand this area is off limits due to danger." His clipped tone informed me that he had heard my comment. "Your presence has been requested by Mr Doyle, my lady. I've brought an umbrella for you both as the heavens are about to open."

I stood up, witnessing what I thought was hurt in Hamilton's gaze. I had no intention of making him feel better since he had clearly brought me over to Moor House as a prospective wife for his employer. I did not reach for the umbrella and walked past Hamilton, taking the steep incline back to the garden as the pitter-patter of rain suddenly became fiercer. Behind me, Freddie chatted to Hamilton in a purring voice, made deep no doubt by her smoking. I imagined she was hanging off his arm as well as his every word.

I sped up, not wishing to hear their exchange. As I reached the garden, Prince bounded up to me followed by Lottie.

Lottie stopped and steadied herself. Her hat was dripping with water and she appeared completely soaked.

"I'm glad we brought a change of clothes," I said. "You can't take luncheon dripping wet."

Lottie shivered. "Prince seems to love it. I couldn't get him to come to me."

My dog barked and looked up at me.

I stepped back, realising what was to come. "Oh no," I said as he shook his coat.

I turned away as Lottie squealed, her dress being sprayed with mud-tinged droplets of water from his coat.

"Thank you, Prince," she said, looking down at

her dress. "You naughty boy." She bent down and stroked him. He licked her face and I smiled. A dose of Lottie's energy and happiness was exactly what I needed. Observing that she was managing to smile through a huge heartbreak, I was sure I could brush away the sad feeling I had about Hamilton, since our relationship amounted to little more than a flirtation.

We stood sheltering under a tree, with Hamilton and Freddie standing beneath a neighbouring one some yards away. With the rain pelting down, I could not hear their conversation and neither did I want to.

"Are you well, Ellen?" Lottie asked as she straightened up with Prince now on his leash. "You look angry."

"I'm fine," I said and attempted a grin.

"You're red." She looked over at Hamilton as Freddie laughed loudly. "Are you jealous of that woman chatting to Ernest?" she said to me as they laughed together.

"Not at all, I'll explain on our way home. We need to change clothes, to get through luncheon and leave as soon as we can."

Lottie raised her eyebrows but said no more.

Hamilton ran over to us and passed an umbrella, which I took with a nod. I shared it with Lottie as we hurried up the lawn with Prince pulling on his leash.

"Ah, there you are," Conrad said as we reached an open door which led into the kitchen.

"Lottie needs to change her clothes," I said, taking Prince's leash from her.

"I'll get them from the motorcar," Lottie said.

"I'll help," I added, realising the trunk would be far too heavy for her.

"I'll fetch it," Hamilton said from behind us, then took Prince's leash.

"Thank you, Ernest," Lottie said.

"Let's you and I go to the drawing room." Conrad offered his arm to me. "Your clothes look relatively dry." He looked at my torso and I took his arm to break his gaze, taking in another waft of his strong aftershave. I gave an inward groan, but decided to be as pleasant as I could muster. I would hopefully only have to endure one more hour with the fellow before heading off.

Conrad led me into the drawing room where a young man in his early twenties with a round face sat in an armchair.

Conrad gestured to him. "My son, Robert Doyle."

The young man stood up. "Pleased to meet you, Lady Ellen. I've heard so much about you, not just from Captain Hamilton but from further afield." He was not as tall as his father and was dressed in a cream suit, which was rather tight across his middle. He had glossy dark hair in the same shade as his sister's. "Men often talk with affection about your convalescent home."

"It's been a busy time," I said with a smile. It appeared that wherever I went, people had often heard of me. I guessed that was because a good few men had stayed at Ashcombe Hall and there would be many in the South West who would have heard of it after their men had returned home.

"Robert will be taking the reins of the family business," Conrad said, gesturing towards the settee for me to be seated.

"I'll be travelling to Egypt to source goods, now we've diversified. Father's hoping to retire next week." He shot a glance at his father. "Assuming his piece sells."

"Of course it will sell," Conrad said with a slight annoyance as if feeling the pressure. "My agent has whipped up a fever amongst art collectors and has already narrowed the list down to the most hungry of buyers."

"How many are coming?" I asked.

"Two a day for three days. They're booked in for either the morning and luncheon or the afternoon and will stay for dinner," Conrad said.

"Father's plan is that none of them meet. It will be a silent auction and the winning bidder will not be made public in order to protect them."

"And why is there a need to be protected?" I asked.

"The piece is valuable and there are thieves around," Conrad said as he scratched his nose.

Freddie entered the room, having changed into a deep red dress. Again, to the floor in an out-dated style. Her wavy hair, glossy from brushing, cascaded over one shoulder.

Lottie followed, also having changed out of her wet clothes, however in a thoroughly modern dress in lilac, which I had bought from a fashion house in Bristol. She wore a matching headband and smiled shyly. "I've left Prince in the scullery with the bone we packed," she said to me.

"This is my companion, Charlotte Penny," I said, realising I had not formally introduced her.

Lottie gave a brief curtsy and Freddie sniggered.

Her brother gave Lottie a broad smile. "I'm Robert Doyle."

"Pleased to meet you, Robert Doyle." She turned to Conrad. "And pleased to meet you Mr Conrad Doyle." Then to Freddie. "And..."

"Yes, yes. We're all awfully pleased to meet you too." Freddie rolled her eyes.

I was beginning to dislike Freddie Doyle and was not fond of her father, either. At least the son appeared pleasant enough. Lottie blushed and I reached for her hand and gave it a brief squeeze of reassurance.

Conrad turned, then addressed a man who entered the room. "Shaw, why have you left the piece unattended?"

The fellow who I placed at about thirty with mousy brown hair gestured outside. "I came to alert you, sir. I've seen a man walking around the periphery of the building."

"So you left a priceless artefact alone?" Conrad boomed, his face turning crimson as he gestured towards Mr Shaw. "Get upstairs, man, and protect the piece!"

Hamilton entered the room, no doubt having heard raised voices.

"On second thoughts," Conrad said. "Hamilton, go up and guard the piece. Shaw, take me to where you saw the fellow." Conrad followed Shaw out of the room when the doorbell chimed. It appeared the visitor had located the entrance. "Who on earth is that?" Conrad said.

Robert appeared agitated and rose from the chair. "We're not expecting anyone for a few days."

"This place is usually so quiet," Freddie said. "It would be nice if something interesting happened."

Chapter Five

In the drawing room, with Robert, Freddie and Lottie, I gestured at a picture of a man upon a racehorse. "Is that one of your father's paintings?" I asked Freddie.

"Heavens, no," she said with a laugh. "I've never seen his artwork. I hope this artefact does raise some money for him as he's not terribly good at anything. I understand his art was mediocre and was locked away when he moved here, in one of the attic rooms." She sighed. "Neither has he a nose for dealing due to incredibly poor taste. He often picks items which are pretty but also pretty worthless." She lit a cigar. "You see, Father is from the working classes and it shows, I'm afraid."

"You are being unkind," Robert said.

"I guess art is often about fashion," I said. "At

Ashcombe Hall, most of our art is either local landscapes or family portraits."

Freddie sighed. "I have to say we've not inherited much here and neither have we been gifted much art. I prefer to work for the women's movement and live within a community in which we all pull together. I have no desire for the trappings of this life," she said.

"That's fortunate, sister dear," Robert said with a laugh.

"Do you live alone?" I asked Freddie.

"No, in a...commune." She gave me a sweet smile.

Robert gave a slow shake of his head.

Freddie frowned at his reaction. "Don't judge me. And just listen to you, how's the vicar's daughter? Are you going to make an honest woman of Grace or are you too seeking a rich wife?"

Robert sighed. "You have no respect, Sister."

"Not for those who don't deserve it," she said, then gestured around the room. "Everything has been in a downward spiral since Mother died. Father's a glorified market trader. He would be better off with a stall in Dulverton market, like Joseph."

"That's enough," Robert said. "And not true."

"I hope for his sake this so-called artefact is indeed worth as much as he thinks it is. It's probably an item picked up at an Egyptian bazaar." She turned to me.

"That's my fear, that Father's been taken advantage of."

"I've seen the piece myself," Robert said. "It's authentic. I've studied Art History at university." He smiled at me.

"Really?" I said trying to sound positive yet feeling a little too warm, through witnessing the siblings disagreement.

We all turned to the door as Conrad entered in a waft of cologne with a man who was, I had to admit, rather dashing with thick rusty hair, damp from the rain. He carried his wet jacket over his shoulder with his shirt undone at the neck.

"May I introduce Lord Purnell," Conrad said, with an obvious annoyance in his voice.

"It appears I'm a little early," Purnell said, instantly fixing his gaze upon me as if he recognised me, and yet I was certain I'd never met the fellow before.

"This is Lady Ellen of Ashcombe Hall," Conrad said. "My guest for the day."

"Welcome to Moor House," Freddie purred as she stepped forward, half in front of me, and appraised Lord Purnell in a manner which made me blush. "Have we met before?" she asked him. "I'm Freddie Doyle."

Purnell took in her face, then put his head to one side. "Bonjour, Madame."

"Bonjour Monsieur. Enchanté," she said in a perfect French accent, then took a step backwards so I had to move to the side to avoid being trodden on. "But it's Mademoiselle." She licked her lips.

Conrad sighed at his daughter's overt display. "I've advised Lord Purnell that he was not expected until at least Friday."

"I seem to have mixed my days up," Purnell said, smiling at me.

"I'll show you upstairs." Conrad turned to Robert. "If you could advise Ivy to serve luncheon, I will join you all as soon as my business concludes."

Conrad turned, but Lord Purnell approached me and took my hand, lifting it to his lips. "It's an honour to meet you at last, Lady Ellen. I've heard so much about you. To find you here is like discovering a priceless gem."

I gulped, feeling as if it was me that Purnell was about to place a bid on. "Have we met before?" I asked in a higher than usual voice.

"Not at all, but many far and wide have heard of you and your good works."

"Please join us after your viewing," Freddie purred at Purnell, with a smile that lit up her face.

"Lord Purnell," Conrad called from the passageway.

Purnell released my hand and left the room.

"Behave, Sister," Robert said once his father and Lord Purnell had left the room.

"He's my type of man. Real, not too preened, with hair you can tousle," Freddie said with a low sigh.

Lottie's eyes shot wide open as well as her mouth.

I leaned forward, lifted her jaw and shook my head at her.

She looked down, realising she needed to work on her manners. Not that Freddie Doyle appeared to be in possession of any, although I chastened myself for being so completely old fashioned. Freddie appeared to be a suffragette and championed equality with men. *I really need to relax*, I thought, *and refrain from being so judgmental.*

"He was simply delicious," Freddie said as if she was starving.

I relaxed slightly, realising this man appealed to Freddie much more than Hamilton did. She was positively salivating over him.

A middle-aged woman entered the drawing room, wearing a blue dress with a crisp apron over the top and carrying a water filled jug. She was tall and attractive with tied back blonde hair interspersed with white. She gave me a curt smile. "Pleased to meet you, Lady Ellen." As she spoke, I noticed a gap between her dazzling teeth. She scanned the room. "I've some lemonade I can bring in if anyone would like a glass?"

I smiled at her and nodded. "Yes please, I love lemonade."

She nodded at me in an efficient manner which was not at all friendly. She had a presence you would not expect from a member of serving staff; they usually blended somewhat into the background but this woman had an air about her. Freddie and Lottie also requested lemonade but she was a lot warmer to them.

After she left the room, I turned to Freddie. "Has your maid worked here long?" I asked, my inquisitiveness getting the better of me.

"Ivy's our housekeeper and cook and has been here since she was twenty-one," Freddie said. "She's Joseph's mother."

Of course, I thought, remembering that Freddie had asked Joseph to tell his mother we were ready for luncheon.

"Always been somewhat fixated with Father," she said with a sigh. "Probably views you as a rival."

"Freddie," Robert said in a cautionary tone.

Ah, I thought, *that explains it.* Ivy Wood did not want her employer to marry again; she wanted to remain the woman of the house.

Freddie nodded out to the garden where Joseph hurried across the lawn. "As I said, Joseph arrived when he was four, so that's twenty years they have been here."

"That's nice, you must have all grown up together," I said.

I noticed Freddie and Robert exchange a glance.

"We were at boarding school for much of our childhood," Robert said.

"Father spent more time with Joseph than either of us!" Freddie said with a sniff.

"Do you have many staff here?" I asked.

Freddie shook her head. "Ivy acts as maid, housekeeper and cook – and no doubt, whatever else Father has a fancy for."

"After Mother died, many staff left," Robert said quickly. "But there's Shaw who acts as butler, footman and gamekeeper."

"And as I said," Freddie added. "Joseph looks after the gardens, including the kitchen garden. It's useful that he can grow food, at least Father will not starve if the artefact turns out to be junk."

"Sister, why do you forever put our father down? I'm sure Lady Ellen finds that quite distasteful," Robert said.

He was completely right, but I made no comment. Being disrespectful of one's parents was not something I condoned, however, neither was I a fan of Conrad Doyle and had little doubt there was an element of truth in his daughter's criticisms of him.

"At least I'm independent and not living off Father." Freddie gave her brother a dismissive wave.

Lottie sat wide-eyed and I nearly laughed at her expression. I hoped that we could soon leave and have a gossip on the way back to Denham Hall about the warring siblings.

"I work the family business." Robert sat up and frowned at his sister.

Freddie ignored him and turned to me. "We had another maid, Grace, but we had to let her go."

Robert stood up, turned his back and poured himself a whisky.

Freddie continued. "She works in town, at the inn, she's the vicar's daughter I mentioned earlier." She looked at Robert as he turned around. "Pretty little thing isn't she, brother dear?"

Robert did not flinch.

Ivy Wood returned and addressed Robert. "Grace is out the back. She's brought the cart with a delivery of refreshments and is just putting the horse in our stable. The poor old nag hates the wet weather."

"Ah, talk of the devil," Freddie said as Robert left the room.

Ivy passed me the promised glass of lemonade. "I hope it's to your liking, my lady."

I wondered what it had been like for her, working

for the Doyles over the years, as I took a sip of the sweet citrus drink. “Delicious,” I said to her.

Lottie nodded in agreement as she drank hers.

“I have to agree,” Freddie said in a low voice.

As I took a second sip, I realised Freddie wasn’t referring to the lemonade at all – the handsome Lord Purnell had returned to the room and again had his eyes upon me. Behind him, Conrad followed with a cheerful expression upon his face. Clearly Purnell had been much impressed with the artefact and had no doubt offered a handsome bid.

There was an element of relief in Conrad’s eyes. “We’ve left Shaw guarding the piece,” he said.

Hamilton followed them in and appeared less cheerful. I sensed he’d had his fill of Conrad Doyle. “Shaw looks hot, as if he could do with some refreshment, it’s stuffy in the attic room,” Hamilton said to Ivy. “I’m sure he’d be grateful for some lemonade if you wish me to deliver him a glass?”

“It’s fine, Captain, I’ll take it up myself,” she said with a dazzling smile that brought a sparkle to her eyes. The gap between her teeth gave her an impish quality.

Conrad gestured at Hamilton. “Can you do another trip around the outside of the house, to make sure the building is secure?”

I watched as Hamilton, with his eyebrows knitted together, turned and left the room. I heard his stick tap furiously on the passageway floor. I was sure the only reason he did not challenge Conrad Doyle was because he felt it rude to cause a scene in front of Lottie and myself. Hamilton was always a complete gentleman and a strong man. I could see no other explanation of why he would remain passive. I gave a small smile. I had to admire his strength of character.

I turned back to Conrad. "You have the item in the attic?" I asked, feeling Lord Purnell's gaze upon me from the corner of my vision.

"It needs to be heavily guarded because, unfortunately, there's been a spate of robberies around here," Conrad said.

"So I heard, a man called The Magpie?" I said. There appeared to be a fashion for allocating criminals nicknames. Such as the Vigilante Slasher who popped up in the newspapers every now and again. He was the most notorious killer of the year. Then there was The Cat, a prominent thief of London hotels, and now The Magpie who had not made the national press but certainly appeared to be making a name for himself locally.

"Is your interest piqued?" Lord Purnell asked me. "Would you like to flush The Magpie out with your detecting skills?" There was a sense of mischievousness in his eyes.

"News travels fast," I said to Lord Purnell, a man I

had never heard of but who apparently knew much about me and the fact that I had unravelled mysteries in Branden Bay. I opened my mouth to continue but was interrupted.

The rude Purnell had turned to Conrad. "I'm intrigued, tell me about this fellow called The Magpie."

Conrad grumbled as he leaned on the mantelpiece. "I was his first victim. He stole my late wife's jewellery."

"I was devastated," Freddie said, looking up at Purnell.

Conrad straightened up. "Luckily it was insured and" – he paused – "she no longer needed it."

"I'm a widower myself. I understand how heart wrenching that must have been," Purnell said in a softer voice and turned, catching my eye before I had the chance to avoid his gaze. Clearly, he knew I was a widow. In that moment, I recognised a flash of grief then tore my eyes away and looked outside as the rain bounced off the stone sun dial in the middle of the lawn. I hoped it subsided as I did not wish to drive home in such conditions. Hamilton ran past the window, taking long strides, his stick thrusting into the lawn. It was almost comical and I felt guilty for thinking so. I knew he was not at all happy.

"It's a stunning piece," Purnell said, pulling my

attention away from the gardens. "Are you bidding on it, my lady?"

"I've not been invited to do so," I said. "I gather it's all rather hush-hush and kept away from those not in the know." I glanced at Conrad Doyle, a man I was beginning to dislike more with every passing moment I spent in his presence. I certainly did not trust him.

"I was not involved with the assessment of potential clients," Conrad commented. "As I said, my agent handled it."

Freddie stood up and faced Purnell with a coy smile. "Would you care for a tour of the rest of the house?"

"No, Freddie. We'll soon be taking luncheon," Conrad said.

I wished it would be served soon, so I could take my leave.

Chapter Six

After polite conversation concerning the dreadful weather, we moved through wide open doors to the dining room, taking our seats as Ivy Wood pushed a fully laden hostess trolley.

Hamilton returned, looking a little bedraggled. He smoothed his hair with his left hand. "I don't expect any more visitors in this weather. The area and house are as secure as they can be."

"Take luncheon with us, Hamilton," Conrad said.

I found myself with Conrad to my left, Lord Purnell to my right and Hamilton opposite scowling. I really did not know what was up with him, after all it was he that brought me there to seemingly entertain his employer. Being on the receiving end of the men each side of me vying for my attention was uncharted waters for me. I looked to Lottie who grinned back. At least the young girl had felt entertained enough to smile, considering her broken heart. This lightened my mood.

"The summer soup is most delicious," Lottie said. She had been practising her elocution with Phoebe's children who were fascinated by Lottie. They loved to play and mimic their last governess and had been giving Lottie lessons. It was highly amusing to watch but had also benefited Lottie, who was trying so hard now to fit into the world to which I had introduced her. To be taking luncheon with us, rather than clearing away the dirty dishes.

"I will pass your compliments to Mrs Wood," Conrad said to her with a smile.

I looked out of the windows with white painted frames to see Joseph taking shelter under a tree as the rain hammered the ground. I hoped that the roof on my car was keeping out the moisture, otherwise I would have to dry the seats before we headed back. *Surely the rain would abate soon,* I thought with an inner sigh.

"So do tell me about your last investigation," Purnell said to me. "I hear at one point you thought you were tracking the Vigilante Slasher?"

"It was the press who considered it was the Slasher," I said. "Not us."

"Lady Ellen realised it was a copycat," Hamilton added, although he was being rather generous with the truth as it had been he who was convinced the death was not undertaken by the Slasher.

"A most intelligent woman," Conrad said from my left.

"And what are your thoughts on the Slasher?" Lord Purnell asked me.

"As I said to Captain Hamilton, two wrongs do not make a right." I took a spoonful of the delicious soup, then ate a piece of Ivy's home baked bread. I missed freshly baked bread for it reminded me of Ashcombe Hall.

"Ah, so Captain Hamilton here approves of the Slasher, does he?" Lord Purnell said.

I saw Hamilton grind his teeth. He clearly did not like Lord Purnell. "I merely pointed out that there are criminals who live under the radar of the police," he said. "They would surely go to the gallows if the police could make a case against them. The Slasher seeks them out."

"Indeed, that's the whole point of calling himself the Vigilante," Purnell said. "It's interesting, Captain, that you approve."

"I never said I approve." Hamilton sat up straight and then wiped his mouth with the napkin. "If you would excuse me, I shall check the servants' door is now locked, as Grace was in the stable." He rose from the table and strode away with his stick tapping on the wooden floor. I guessed Hamilton had had his fill of both Conrad and Purnell.

"What did the fellow do to his leg?" Conrad asked me.

I knew that Hamilton carried the stick as a mental crutch and that his affliction was shell shock. He said that once he was rid of the nightmares and flashbacks, he would return the stick to me. I had given it to him six years previously, whilst he was a patient at my convalescent home, and the stick had belonged to my papa.

"I don't think Captain Hamilton would appreciate us talking about him," I said. "You may wish to ask him yourself."

"I already have, but the chap changes the subject whenever I do." Conrad wiped his mouth with his napkin.

"That's because he don't want you to know!" Lottie said, without her learned pronunciation. She was clearly put out by the men discussing Hamilton, who she had much regard for.

I could not help a small laugh escaping me. Lottie did so cheer me up and lighten my mood. "Where did you acquire your Egyptian artefact?" I quickly interjected to change the subject and cover up Lottie's faux pas.

Conrad glanced at Lord Purnell. "I cannot divulge that information."

"Did you admire the piece, Lord Purnell?" I asked. "I'd love you to describe it to me."

He glanced at Conrad. "It's a silent auction and I've signed something to say I will not discuss it."

"Oh dear," I said. "I'm beginning to wonder if this is all above board."

I glanced to my side to see Conrad's face turn a deep shade of red, but he made no comment.

"It's to protect the new owner, my dear," Lord Purnell said in a patronising manner, as if a woman would not understand. But I understood perfectly, even if Conrad was pulling the wool over Lord Purnell's eyes. There was something not quite right about this piece and I was most surprised that an upstanding gentleman such as Captain Hamilton had agreed to protect it.

Prince's bark echoed in the distance.

I reached for my napkin and dabbed my lips, then took a deep breath. "If you will excuse me, gentlemen, it appears that my dog is restless." I stood up. "The rain has subsided. I will take Prince for a turn in the gardens before I make my return trip. Come along, Lottie, we will all stretch our legs. Thank you for the meal."

"I can't wait to leave," I whispered to Lottie as we

walked along the passageway to fetch Prince from the scullery. "This trip was a mistake."

"I don't think Ernest is happy," Lottie said.

"I'm the one who's unhappy, with him bringing me here because his employer is looking for a wealthy wife!" My voice had increased in volume and I reminded myself to not display my distaste.

Lottie gasped. "Ernest would never do that, Ellen. I'm sure it's a misunderstanding. I don't like that Mr Doyle, it's all his fault."

I turned to her and saw a tear in her eye and remembered she was sensitive and also held Hamilton in high regard. Her words were rather sensible; I had let my emotions run away with me.

"I'm sorry. You're right. I'll speak to Ernest before we leave," I said as we reached the scullery and Prince approached us with his tail wagging so fiercely his hind was moving from side to side.

The rain had subsided, although the sky appeared to be darkening. I guessed this was a short reprieve. "Once Prince has had a run, we'll check the motorcar for leaks," I said.

We had only covered half of the lawn before a cloud burst, followed by a clap of thunder. I spotted the gardener's shed and gestured towards it. We both hurried down a gravel path to the door, but unfortunately found it locked. The rain became heavier. I pointed to a large tree and we ran towards it. I could not face returning to the house.

The rain pelted down and we stood with our backs pressed against the bark of the oak tree.

"I think I'm going to get this dress soaked as well," Lottie said in a loud voice to be heard. "I'm glad we brought extra for choice."

Prince jumped around on the grass and we laughed at him. He had always loved the water and often took a dip in the stream, ponds and small lake back at the Ashcombe Estate. I felt myself calm as I watched him. My gaze moved to the house beyond him. Hamilton appeared at the kitchen door and waved at us. I took a deep breath and gave him a small wave back. Maybe Lottie was right and it was a misunderstanding.

We waited whilst the rain fell. I was sure I had never seen weather like it. It was as if a year's worth of rain fell in ten minutes. Water streamed down the grassy slope towards us and my shoes were soon filled. There followed a flash and a clap of thunder.

"We need to return to the house," I shouted above the torrent. "We can't stand within the trees in a storm."

I looked up to see Hamilton striding out of the house and down the small slope, through the sodden grass towards us, slipping at times and using his stick for the purpose it was designed for. Prince stood in the middle of the lawn, shaking the water from his coat.

"Ellen," Hamilton said as he reached us and the rain eased.

"I'll head into the house and change," Lottie said. "I have one more dry dress." I knew she simply wanted to give Hamilton and myself some time alone. "Hello," she added to Hamilton before hurrying up the lawn towards the house. She ran off with her head down as the rain returned.

Prince bounded up to Hamilton and ran around him before stopping to be petted. Hamilton stroked his damp head. "You're always pleased to see me." He turned to me and spoke loudly over the top of the weather. "Ellen, I must explain that I did not invite you here to spend the time being pestered by Conrad Doyle and his associate."

I felt the tension leave my body. I had not realised until that moment how much I needed to hear those words from him. I felt unable to speak.

He continued. "Conrad invited you and Lottie to accompany myself to what he described as a garden party and then, as you know, made sure I was absent so he could monopolise you."

I made no further comment but a small smile formed on my face.

Hamilton continued. "I'm also unhappy with

Conrad's arrangement for auctioning this artefact. It doesn't sit right with me. I've decided to end my contract to provide security services to Doyle and will no longer guard the piece. I doubt whether I will see a penny from him."

"Please don't do that on my account, Ernest. I've already ruined a few jobs for you. And you've not accepted anything from me in compensation." Hamilton had already cancelled contracts to help me with my investigations. "Although I too am rather nervous that this artefact may not have been acquired in a lawful manner."

"I wish to distance myself from the man," Hamilton added.

"Would you care for a trip to Denham Hall?" I asked him as relief washed over me. "You will have to sit in the back with Prince, I'm afraid."

Hamilton laughed. "I'm more than happy with that." He visibly relaxed. "I will not impose. If you drop me at Tiverton I will find lodgings and transport for my onward journey."

"I'm sure Lady Denham will be only too pleased to have you visit her with us. Phoebe has said on a few occasions that she's dying to meet you and she will not forgive me if I leave you stranded in Tiverton. Apart from that, I would love for you to accompany us to Denham Hall." I gave him an encouraging smile.

"If it pleases you, Ellen." He looked into my eyes.

I felt my face flush as the sound of the water upon the leaves calmed me and I felt the tight knot which had constricted my body melt away. I was with Hamilton and we would soon be safely back at Denham Hall where we could relax and speak freely, away from the awful Doyle family and the unnerving Lord Purnell.

The rain finally stopped and a calmness followed as if the birds and wildlife were debating whether it was safe to step out of the cosy shelter they had no doubt found themselves. I took a step forward, then jumped. There was a bright flash and an immediate clap of thunder. We heard a distant creek and crash. And then the sounds of a horse whinnying.

"Sounds like a tree being felled," Hamilton said, looking in the direction of the river. "I'll check your motorcar before the heavens open again to ensure it has not taken in water." Hamilton looked down at me with a warm smile. "You had better get into the house in case of any more lightning strikes."

I turned towards the house. I could not wait to leave the premises, but then I stopped still and gasped. On the doorstep was the housekeeper Ivy Wood, with crimson blood on her hands and splashes of it on her crisp white apron.

"Joseph," she screamed.

Chapter Seven

Hamilton raced up the slope of the lawn and I took the path, not wishing to slip, with my head down as the heavens opened yet again. Prince bounded ahead of us. When we reached Ivy, she was in hysterics on the kitchen doorstep. Prince stopped and whined and I gave his back a stroke. With Hamilton's help I took Ivy inside and sat her down at the kitchen table before I searched her body for a wound.

As I checked her, she wiped her forehead, leaving a swipe of crimson upon her pale skin.

"Have you any pain?" I asked in the calmest voice I could muster.

Freddie entered the room. "I heard screaming. Whatever's the matter, Ivy?" She put a hand on her shoulder. She looked at the vegetable prep on the table and then back at the cook. "Have you cut yourself?"

Ivy gasped and Hamilton asked her to take regular breaths as I continued to examine her. I stepped back as it soon became apparent that the blood was not coming from her person.

"I want Joseph. He must be in his shed," Ivy said. "Joseph," she called out with a wail.

"Mrs Wood, you must tell us where you have been wounded," Hamilton said.

"It's not her blood," I said to Freddie and Hamilton. I gulped then turned back to Mrs Wood. "Who's injured?"

Freddie stopped rubbing Ivy's shoulder. "Have you hurt someone?" she asked then touched her own neck.

"Shaw," Ivy said in a shuddering voice.

Conrad burst into the room. "It's gone!" He paced the kitchen, his eyes wild.

Joseph entered the room behind him. "What's the matter?" He walked past Conrad to his mother. "Ma, you're hurt?" he asked her with fear in his eyes.

Ivy shook her head and burst into tears. "It's Shaw, he's been stabbed."

"Is the artefact missing?" Hamilton asked Conrad.

Lottie came into the kitchen. "What's wrong?" she asked. Prince rushed up to her from the back door and barked, clearly upset.

"Someone has stabbed Shaw and stolen my artefact," Conrad said. "Purnell is up there with him, trying to stem the flow of blood. I've come down to ask Robert to drive the motorcar to town and fetch Doctor Jones."

Robert Doyle entered with a young woman who had a blonde bob and I assumed was Grace, the vicar's daughter who worked at the inn.

"What's all the commotion about?" Robert asked.

"Grace, fetch some brandy for Ivy?" Freddie said to her.

Grace left the room.

"Get the doctor," Conrad said to his son. "The artefact's gone. Shaw's been stabbed. Quick, take the motorcar."

Robert left the room and Grace soon returned and handed a brandy bottle and glass to Freddie, who filled the tumbler with a shaky hand and passed it to Ivy.

Conrad turned to leave the room.

"Let me see Shaw," I called out. "I can help before the doctor arrives."

Conrad turned his head and frowned at me. "It's not a scene for a lady." He turned to Hamilton. "Come with me."

Hamilton followed him out.

I stood for a moment, watching them go, then turned back into the room. "I'm going up to the attic," I said to Lottie. "Can you keep an eye on Prince?"

"But Ellen, it might be dangerous," Lottie said.

"I've experience of treating the wounded," I said. And neither was I pleased at being ordered around by the men.

"Of course, yes," Lottie said.

"It may take some time for the doctor to arrive with the bad weather," I added.

"I'll show you the way," Freddie said then turned to Grace. "Stay with Ivy." She took the bottle of brandy from the table and grabbed a clean cup from a hook.

"I'll make you some sweet tea," Lottie said to Ivy, who was sobbing with Joseph comforting her as we left.

I wanted to leave Moor House and return to Denham Hall and tell Phoebe about the miserable day I'd had but knew I could not leave a man to bleed out whilst he waited for medical assistance. I was trained and although I had not practised for some months, I would always be a nurse at heart.

Outside of the kitchen, Freddie passed me and took a right turn. I followed her along the corridor until I came to a flight of steps which I took, hearing the voices of the men pounding the stairs above. Once on the landing, we took the additional flight of stairs to the attic.

"Have you telephoned the doctor?" Lord Purnell asked Conrad as we entered the room.

"We don't have a telephone service here. I've sent Robert in my motorcar to fetch him from Dulverton."

Shaw moaned.

"Let me check him," I said as I stepped inside the room, viewing the poor man and the blood splattered rug. He was losing a lot of blood.

"Ellen, this is not for your eyes," Hamilton said with concern.

Lord Purnell was hunched over Shaw's body. "I agree," he said in a grim voice.

"Give the man space to breathe," I ordered.

"Lady Ellen, maybe you would prefer to console Mrs Wood, downstairs," Lord Purnell said as he looked up at me.

I put my hands upon my hips, in the way my housekeeper, Dawkins back at Ashcombe Hall, did when addressing junior staff who would not do as they were told. "I can assure you I've seen worse." I gestured at my host. "I'm a trained nurse."

"Do as Lady Ellen says," Hamilton said, then smiled at me. "Apologies, Ellen."

Purnell rose to his full height and Conrad stood back.

As I approached Shaw, the rain was again drumming on the roof and water was coming into the room from the open window. I could not believe the sky held any more rain to fall.

I knelt beside the bleeding man and appraised the wound in his right side. "It's not that deep," I said. "We simply need to stop the flow. He's lucky, I don't think it's in a place where there's a vital organ." I addressed Shaw directly even though his eyes were closed. "You're going to be fine."

Shaw groaned.

"Who was it man?" Conrad demanded, realising his butler was conscious.

He murmured but it was unintelligible.

"I'm afraid we need to keep the man comfortable and quiet," I said. "High blood pressure and stress could make matters much worse. Please, Mr Doyle, your questioning will have to wait." I felt pleased that I was now in a dominant position with the man, even if the circumstances were most unfortunate.

Conrad paced the room. "This is not good. That's my whole life down the drain if we don't find it." It was clear that Conrad had more concern for his stolen artefact than his faithful employee.

"I need hot water, clean cloths, iodine if you have it, if not, alcohol – whisky will do. Also petroleum jelly, scissors and aspirin," I said to Freddie who was at the door, staring at Shaw on the ground with her hand to her neck. Her face was ashen and she had remained by the door, quiet, displaying her human side. She nodded before leaving to do my bidding.

"I need a handkerchief to stem the flow." The cloth they had been using was no longer adequate.

Hamilton handed me his and I attended to Shaw again, who appeared to now be unconscious.

Conrad gestured out of the window. "The fire rope has been dropped and it has blood on it." He left this way. He turned back and gestured at Lord Purnell. "Was it you?"

"Calm down, Doyle," Purnell said. "I can assure you if I'd stabbed the man and stolen the" – he glanced at me, seemingly being careful not to describe the piece – "item, I would have left already."

"The exits were well protected," Hamilton said.

"I managed to get in," Purnell pointed out with his eyebrows raised. "The security here is hardly as tight as the Tower of London. Anyone could have got in."

Hamilton's eyes fixed upon him and for a split second I thought there was going to be a tussle between the pair.

"It's not your fault, Captain Hamilton," I said. "No one could make this place totally secure, not with it being surrounded by woods."

Hamilton took a breath and stepped back without commenting.

I turned to him, feeling he needed some space to calm down. "Could you help Freddie fetch the items from the kitchen and remind her the water will need to be boiled first."

Hamilton nodded. "Certainly." He left the room.

Shaw groaned as I applied pressure to the wound with Hamilton's handkerchief. He opened his eyes. "The Magpie," he gasped, then shut them again.

"I knew it," Conrad said. "The blighter has stolen from me again!"

"Well, I never," Lord Purnell said. He gestured to the open window. "He must have come in through there in broad daylight."

I presumed The Magpie was long gone. As soon as this wound was dressed and the doctor had arrived, I intended to leave. Mystery or no mystery, I'd had enough excitement for one summer and needed to relax. And this was one case I would gladly leave to the police. Although part of me doubted Conrad would alert them, if the artefact had been acquired from suspicious sources.

After what felt like forever, Hamilton and Freddie arrived with the water and dressings. Shaw flinched as I treated him. It must have been painful for the poor man. After I'd dressed the wound, Hamilton and Purnell carried a moaning Shaw down the narrow staircase to a bedroom which Ivy Wood, who had since composed herself, had prepared for him.

"There's a triple layer of fresh sheets," she said to me.

"I've stemmed the flow of blood," I said.

"Shall I clean upstairs?" Freddie asked. Her brazen nature had disappeared, and she seemed genuinely shaken.

"The police will not want that," I said, not looking for Conrad's reaction.

"Police?" he asked. "They're useless. They didn't find The Magpie the first time and won't this time. It's such an upheaval, I won't bother with them."

I ignored his words. This wasn't simply a robbery – a man had been stabbed. I decided I would inform the police myself on my way to Denham. "They'll want to see the scene as it is."

"I'll stay with Shaw," Freddie said, seemingly agreeing that cleaning up the attic was not a good idea.

"I'll wash, if I may," Ivy said in a quiet voice. Whilst she had washed her hands and changed her clothes, there was still a trace of blood in her hair.

"Let us go to the kitchen and have tea," I said.

"We'll send the doctor up as soon as he arrives," Conrad said. "And don't mention it to anyone outside this house." He looked at all of us. "Do you understand?"

On our way down the stairs, I met Lottie on her way up.

"Shaw's in bed now," I said to her. "I've dressed the wound, it's not that deep but he lost some blood. He's probably a little dizzy because of that. We're going to drink tea."

As we reached the kitchen, we found a rather bedraggled Robert waiting there with Grace.

"Where's Doctor Jones?" Conrad asked him.

"The river has burst its banks," Robert said, his face ashen as he drank his brandy. "The road is flooded and a tree has fallen on top of the bridge which has likely damaged it. It's impassable. We can't get to Dulverton until they move the tree and check the bridge is safe to cross."

"What?" Conrad said. "You can't even get over it on foot?"

"Someone agile may well be able to, but there would be risk of injury. Certainly Doctor Jones wouldn't be able to cope at his age."

Grace was red faced. "No one can come here or leave."

My shoulders drooped. It was not just Robert that reached for the brandy. Myself and Lottie also had a glass to calm our nerves.

After we had emptied our glasses, I took a deep

breath and Lottie reached for my hand. I gave her a weary smile as she squeezed it.

"Where's Shaw?" Robert asked.

"In the Rose Room," Conrad said. "If the river is impassable, The Magpie could still be on our land. Hamilton, Purnell. Check the grounds!"

Purnell raised his eyebrows. I assumed he was not used to being ordered around by a man of a much lower class. But he did not protest.

"I'll go clockwise," Hamilton said to the lord. "You go the other way and we'll meet in the middle." The way he looked at Purnell, it sounded as if he was arranging a duel!

Conrad turned to me in a gentler tone. "Lady Ellen, please accompany me to my study."

I took a deep breath, for I knew what was coming, but I followed him as requested, leaving Lottie to check on Prince who was again in the scullery. The study was two doors down the corridor. As we entered the room, Conrad spun around.

"Lady Ellen, please, you have to discover what has happened to the artefact."

"I think really, you need to call upon the police!" I said. "I'm sure they will clear the bridge as soon as possible if they know there's been a stabbing here in this house!"

"No! No police." He lowered his voice as he closed the door and then walked around his desk and sat down. He took a deep breath and motioned for me to sit opposite him. "I'm sorry." He smoothed his hair with his right hand. "Hamilton spoke of you most highly." He poured himself a whisky from a cut glass decanter upon his desk. "So, will you? I understand you never accept payment."

I've never been offered any, I thought. The gall of this man, not only wanting a rich wife, but also expecting everything for free.

He continued. "We're marooned until they clear the bridge. Last time it was damaged, it took a few days. Please, I need my artefact back!"

I sighed. "The thief will be long gone."

He took a deep breath. "I don't trust anyone."

I frowned. "You think it could be someone in this house?"

"Anyone could wear black and pretend to be The Magpie." He stood up. "Although I'm probably being paranoid." He downed his drink then turned to face me. "I want your help. I'm desperate, I need to feel I've done as much as I can to get it back. That I at least tried." He placed his glass on the table.

"I would rather not," I said. "But if I do have any observations whilst I am trapped here, I will of course report them to you. However, as soon as the bridge is fixed, I will be leaving. I do not wish to be involved.

My senses are telling me your item was not above board."

"It was purchased in good faith, my lady, but I understand your reservations. And I think it safer if I do not divulge to you what the item is at this stage."

"You wish me to search for an item and I am not being told what it looks like?" I shook my head in disbelief.

"I apologise for these unfortunate circumstances and am most grateful for anything you discover," he said, ignoring my comment. He reached for the decanter and topped up his glass. "I've lost everything. I'm a failed man. I lost my gift to paint, I lost my wife, I've wasted the family fortune and now the last attempt at making back some of what I've lost has failed."

"You have this house?" I said, sightly touched by his honesty about his weaknesses.

He turned and gave me a rueful look. "How would it look if I sold the house and moved away? Losing the Firth family home which should go to my children when I die." He sighed. "My wife looked after the place. Poor Winnie, if I had been here that day, I might have saved her and she would still be here." He took a deep breath. "To look after her weak husband."

The animosity I had felt for him softened. I saw a man admitting his failings and it was something I had witnessed many times at the convalescent home. At least he was taking responsibility for the position he was in and not blaming third parties, even if a thief was at play. *No,* I told myself. *Don't get sucked in.* But try as I might to distance myself, I knew deep down that I had been presented with my next case.

Chapter Eight

Considering it was summer, Moor House had a chill about it, and I guessed that a few of the inhabitants were suffering with some level of shock. Hamilton and Purnell had returned, reporting no sight of intruders or evidence that someone had exited the property, but even Conrad conceded that trying to keep a tight security on such a property, surrounded by woods, was fruitless.

In the drawing room, Conrad stood by the unlit fireplace smoking a cigarette. Myself and Lottie sat on a settee in the bay window with Prince at our feet. Freddie and Robert were sitting on another settee opposite us. Ivy Wood entered the room with a tray of drinks and Hamilton gallantly helped her to serve them to us, whilst Purnell read a book from Conrad's bookshelf. He was the least bothered by the situation, which was to be expected considering he was neither family nor friend. He looked up from his book every now and again and gave me an amused smile. I had the impression that Lord Purnell was enjoying this whole escapade. Freddie smiled up at him longingly. Since she had overcome the shock of seeing Shaw injured, she'd returned to her brazen self and gazing at Purnell appeared to put her in better spirits. I felt a sense of relief that her attention had moved away from Hamilton.

Lottie leaned over the padded armrest as she gazed out of the side of the bay window. Quieter than usual, I was not sure whether it was because she missed Sebastian or that she felt intimidated by the personalities in the room. Prince gave one low woof and Lottie turned to scratch his tummy as he rolled around on the rug. His deep auburn fur was dry and he was enjoying being fussed over.

The gardener Joseph and Grace entered the room and sat in singular chars set against the wall. Conrad had sent word around for us all to gather together.

"My father will be angry that I'm here," Grace complained. "And the inn will be short staffed."

"It's not your fault, is it?" Robert said. "If you're marooned here with the bridge blocked." He gave her a small smile from across the room.

She smiled back then looked to Conrad and her

face dropped. His expression was filled with disapproval.

"If we could all be quiet," Conrad said. A hush fell as he gained everyone's attention. "Please take a seat," he said, gesturing to Hamilton and Ivy. Purnell remained standing, leaning against the bookcase. "I've asked you all here as I have an announcement to make." Conrad looked around the room and then rested his gaze upon me. "I have appointed Lady Ellen to investigate this matter. If you could please give her your full cooperation." He nodded at me with a half-smile.

Oh, I thought, assuming he wanted me to give a speech and I looked to Lottie. She gave me an encouraging smile but I felt somewhat lost for words. The room fell silent as I looked around at those present. Firstly, Conrad Doyle, my host who appeared extremely stressed as he sucked hard on his cigarette before puffing the smoky air from his lungs, which mixed with the heady aroma of strong cologne. Ivy Wood, the housekeeper, had placed a seat next to her son, Joseph, and twisted her handkerchief in her hand. Joseph stared downwards, picking at the work-rough skin on his palms. Blonde Grace, the vicar's daughter, appeared worried and I wondered whether she had even told her family that she was visiting Moor House. Robert, the man she clearly loved, held an expression which was dark as he regarded his father. Freddie sat puffing on her cigar whilst looking down her nose at her brother with intermittent gazes at Purnell. My eyes rested on Hamilton, who gave me a smile of encouragement which filled me with a measure of self-belief – until my gaze finally rested on Lord Purnell. He stood, leaning against the bookcase with his arms crossed, eyeing me with what looked like amusement as if anticipating my words.

Purnell stood to attention and uncrossed his arms. "So, what does the great detective *Mrs* Ellen Tamar deduce?"

I frowned. Purnell had used my married name. I knew it was to somehow put me down, to emphasise the fact that my title was a courtesy title handed to me by my father and I did not hold a title myself, as he clearly did. Lord Purnell might already be an earl, or a duke as far as I knew. I had no knowledge of the man or his heredity and was certainly not interested enough to ask. But I knew one thing: if this Lord Purnell was seeking to undermine me, it was for a reason. In that moment, I deduced that he felt threatened by me in some way and heard my housekeeper's voice in my head. *I'm having none of that!* An expression she used when feeling attacked by another. I realised I missed Dawkins and was hit by a sudden pang of homesickness. She had always been in my life. Always picked me up and made me strong when I felt weak, when Mama died, when Papa died, when war struck and when Leo passed, even if she did it without visible affection.

"Well then?" Purnell said, as I realised I had the attention of the room and was lost within my thoughts.

I breathed in some of Dawkins's energy, ignored Purnell's comment and addressed the room. "I will simply make observations whilst I'm here, which may help discover what happened to the artefact and who took it."

"Didn't Shaw say it was The Magpie?" Ivy Wood said with a shaky voice.

"It's hardly likely to be one of us, is it. We're all where we're supposed to be," Robert said. "Well apart from our surprise guest." He shot a glance at Purnell.

Purnell put a hand to his chest with a sparkle in his eye. "How exciting, I'm a suspect." He stared at me.

"Do you think it was The Magpie?" Conrad asked Hamilton. "Shaw seems to think it was."

"I do not have detailed knowledge of The Magpie," Hamilton said. "Only what you have told me yourself."

"Maybe someone would like to enlighten us?" I said, looking at Purnell.

Purnell laughed. "I've no idea, I rarely visit Dulverton."

Freddie swished her hair over her shoulder. "He

dresses in black, covers his face with a dark scarf, wears a black woollen hat, scales buildings and steals whilst his victims sleep."

"It won't be him," Robert said. "I've not heard of him stealing artefacts, merely simple jewellery. Items he can sell on, not items of immeasurable wealth. And as I understand it, no locals know of the auction, isn't that right, Father?"

Conrad nodded. "Only select collectors of great wealth have been contacted." He glanced at Purnell. "I used an agent in London, I've no idea myself of who is due to arrive as the agent has yet to send me the final list, which will be here before the correct arrival date."

"So, it could really be anyone, if you have people showing up from across the country?" Purnell said.

"The sale was not due to commence yet. Why was it again you turned up so early?" Robert asked him in a voice laden with accusation.

Purnell shrugged. "I misheard. It happens. I'd been sea swimming before taking the call and had probably retained water in my ear." He flashed me a mischievous smile. This was a man who was certainly lying.

"The Magpie would have come here if he heard there was something worth stealing," Conrad said. "Of course he would have. If he could sell it, he'd never have to steal again." Conrad pointed around the room.

"Which one of you has spoken to the locals about the artefact?"

"I've spoken to no one of it," Joseph said as Conrad's gaze fell on him. "I don't talk with folks about matters that don't concern me or them and I don't even know what this artefact is that you speak of."

"Me neither," Ivy said. "To be honest, I wasn't even interested."

"And I've not mentioned the amulet to any of our contacts," Robert said.

"Amulet?" Freddie asked.

"Robert." Conrad glowered at his son. "You weren't supposed to..."

"Sorry, Father." Robert puffed out and shook his head as if berating himself.

"You slipped up," Purnell said with a laugh, then turned to me. "It's a beautiful piece. Shame it's gone, I rather wanted it in my Egyptian collection." He smiled at me and I doubted whether he had any such collection.

"Who have you told?" Conrad pointed to his son.

"No one," Robert said.

"Did you tell your little *friend* here?" Conrad approached Grace, who was at this stage flushing red. "You've a loose tongue and you work in the inn and..." He pointed to his son. "Don't think that it has escaped my attention what you two are up to!"

"I've said nothing, to no one," Grace stuttered. Again, someone else I considered to be lying.

"But you knew about it?" Conrad demanded.

Grace gave a sideways glance to Robert. Clearly she did not want to get him into trouble with his father, but it was apparent to me she was well aware of the nature of the missing item.

Conrad glared at his son. "You told Grace. Look at her face!" He gestured at the young woman.

Grace stared at her hands which were placed on her lap and bit her lip.

"So you've already lied to me," Conrad gestured at Robert. "And you wanted to take over the business? You've no idea about confidentiality. You'll never succeed in business. You may as well get a job at the inn with your girlfriend."

"Calm down, Father," Robert said. "No one will help you find the person who stole from you if you bully them."

Conrad huffed and walked back to the fireplace, threw his cigarette stub into the bare hearth and lit another.

"We need calm," I said. "Hopefully, tomorrow the police will be able to reach the house and shed some light on this Magpie fellow and whether they think it has similar elements to his other crimes." I had no desire to track down a local thief who had evaded the police for some months.

Conrad swung around. "I said, no police!" He stared at me. His eye twitched.

"Please show some respect to Lady Ellen," Hamilton said. "And why do you want no police? Was the piece illegally acquired?"

"Um," Conrad said.

Purnell laughed. "The fashion of the sale, with this anonymous silent auction, certainly suggests it was not entirely above board."

"So you're happy with buying stolen goods are you, Lord Purnell?" I asked him. "Considering you've come all this way to view the item."

He hesitated, then said no more, giving me a smile and a nod as if he respected my line of questioning. Which was odd; he seemed far from bothered that he may be accused of robbery and grievous harm to the butler.

"When I bought the amulet, it was *not* stolen goods," Conrad blustered. "I bought it from a registered dealer."

"Of course it was stolen," Freddie said and stood up, placing a hand upon her hip. Her dress swished as she took two paces towards her father, then gestured at him with her cigar. "I consider that all of the pieces taken from the tombs are stolen goods. They should be left where they are."

"Bravo!" Purnell said with a laugh, clearly enjoying Freddie's theatrics.

Freddie shot him a broad smile.

"Sit down, Sister, with your fake morals," Robert said.

Lottie looked wide-eyed as the family warred. I patted her hand. Prince had stopped his playful rolling and was sitting to attention, his left ear cocked as if guarding us.

"Where did you acquire the amulet?" I asked Conrad. "I'm curious."

"From a chap I met when doing business in Bristol," he said.

"Who?" Hamilton asked.

Conrad remained silent.

"You have to tell us, man. So we know what we're dealing with," Hamilton added.

"Donny Fingo," Conrad said in a small voice.

"The crime lord?" I said.

"Isn't he dead?" Lottie asked.

Purnell stepped forward. "Indeed, he fell victim to the Vigilante Slasher." He stared at Hamilton and then to me.

"And his brother was killed too," Grace added. "I read about it a couple of weeks ago in the newspaper."

"Fingo told me he bought it at the docks from the shipment which came in from Egypt," Conrad said.

Purnell gave a short and sarcastic laugh, clearly finding the whole episode thoroughly entertaining. "The Fingo brothers were the biggest crooks in Bristol. They made the smugglers in Cornwall look like petty thieves."

"True," Freddie said and sat back down.

"They were art traders," Hamilton said, seeming not to appreciate Purnell's response. "It was a cover for their illegal operations." He looked to Conrad. "I understand the Fingos' art business was by the book and it's since been taken over by law-abiding members of their family."

I looked to Hamilton. "How do you know that?"

"I have contacts in Bristol." Hamilton took a deep breath. "But Donny Fingo was still a crook and traded in many black market goods."

Lord Purnell took a step towards him. "So you knew him well, did you, Captain?"

"I never met the man," Hamilton said. "As I said, I have mutual business contacts and read the extensive newspaper reports about the Slasher."

"Do you think the Fingos deserved to die?" Purnell asked, staring at Hamilton and not letting the matter drop.

Is he trying to push the attention away from himself? My dislike for Lord Purnell was increasing.

"Stop this," Conrad said with a raised voice. "If you would be so kind as to take a seat Lord Purnell and listen to what our esteemed guest, Lady Ellen, has to say on the matter."

I looked to Conrad. I really did not want to take responsibly for this whole case. "If you wish me to investigate, it is necessary for me to question your wish for the police not to be involved," I said, knowing Conrad would have preferred me to ask him that in private. I was feeling very much an imposter as far as being a detective was concerned. "I have no wish to become embroiled in something illegal," I added when he did not immediately reply.

"I've already said, it was legal. But I don't want the police involved, they'll draw attention to what's supposed to be a private sale." Conrad sat down between his son and daughter.

Robert addressed me. "Many Egyptian artefacts are on the market for sale," he said. "They come into Bristol every week. Father bought the item honestly. It seems this is a distraction." He stared at Purnell. "I don't believe it's The Magpie, I believe it's someone masquerading as him."

Conrad put his head into his hands. "If any of you have it...please return it." He looked up and scanned the room. "I spent the last of our capital on it, we have nothing left apart from the house and grounds. I need to locate it otherwise I will no longer be able to afford the wage bill and may have to sell the house."

Freddie groaned. "Father, you idiot."

"Mr Doyle," Joseph said. "Me and Ma will always be here for you. I can put food on your table."

Ivy remained silent, watching on, her gaze constantly fixed on Conrad.

Freddie gave a slow clap. "Oh, listen to the doting employee," she hissed. "Forever tied to your mother's apron strings. A mother who no doubt would do *anything* for my dear father." She gave a short laugh. Any compassion I had seen in Freddie earlier on had been obliterated. However, I deduced from her comments and the blush which had now formed on Ivy's face that the housekeeper indeed had an affection for Mr Doyle that transcended the master-servant relationship.

"We are merely faithful employees," Ivy said in a brusque fashion as if the bad behaviour of the Doyles was bringing her back to life. "Joseph does more for your father than you do. And he knows how to show him respect."

Freddie laughed. "We all know that you would prefer for us to be out of the way."

I exchanged a look with Lottie. There appeared to be much said between the lines.

Ivy stood up. "I'll check on Shaw. We should not leave him alone." She left the room. I wished I could follow her as the tension in the room was quite unpleasant.

I broke the silence. "I think we need to take a breath. We're stranded here. If it was this Magpie fellow, he's probably in the woods somewhere hiding. If he can scale buildings, he will be more than capable of climbing over a tree." I much preferred that theory than to think the thief was sitting in the drawing room.

Conrad sighed. "It's gone, I can feel it." He looked up. "Hamilton, please check the outbuildings to see if there's any sign of an intruder." He gestured at Joseph. "You go with him."

"Of course," Joseph said as he stood up.

"I shall do this for you," Hamilton said. "But I'm no longer working for you Mr Doyle, please make note of that." He turned to me. "I'm happy to be of help to you in any way I can, Lady Ellen."

"Thank you. You may wish to take Prince with you," I said, knowing my dog would protect him and sniff out any intruder.

Lottie handed Hamilton the leash.

"I'll help prepare the evening meal," Grace said in

a small voice as if returning to her previous role in the house.

"I'll come too," Lottie said, smiling at her.

"I'll relieve Ivy so she can return to the kitchen," Freddie said, looking at Grace and Lottie then flaring her nostrils. "We want something edible."

Conrad gestured towards his son. "I need to have a private talk with you." Robert followed him out of the room.

I therefore found myself alone with Lord Purnell.

Chapter Nine

As I stood in the drawing room, Lord Purnell stared at me with amusement in his eyes. "I must say, this is thoroughly entertaining."

"That a man has been stabbed?" I asked. "He could have died."

"He'll live, don't be so dramatic. You're so uptight, Mrs Tamar."

I refused to challenge him over the way he addressed me. I did not want him to succeed in belittling me. To be honest, I would have given anything to be called Mrs Tamar if it meant my dear Leonard was still alive. Although the title was a link to my beloved Papa, and gave me the means to help others in the way I wished, I had no real attachment to it.

"Why did you want the amulet so much to come here and bid on it?" I asked him.

"Everyone's interested in Egyptian artefacts, Ellen."

I baulked at his familiarity but ignored his continuous attempt to get underneath my skin.

"I'm also enjoying your company," he said. "Someone of my own class."

"I've heard the name Purnell, somewhere before," I said. "But I can't place it." *Maybe he's The Magpie,* I thought. "Where abouts are you situated?" I asked.

"Cornwall. On the coast," he said, clearly not wishing to elaborate – there was a lot of coast in Cornwall, which led me to think he was probably lying.

"Where were you exactly when the amulet was stolen?" I asked him.

He stared at me as if studying my face. "I do believe you're interrogating me."

"Where were you?" I repeated.

He gestured around the room. "I was in here, reading a book. It was a book on anatomy, very detailed about the human body." He gave me a mischievous look up and down as if assessing my physique.

"Really, Lord Purnell!" I said.

He laughed. "But!" He paused, then spoke in a whisper. "I was on my own." He widened his eyes in mock surprise and he took a step back. "And have no alibi."

"Clearly you're not taking the matter seriously. A

priceless artefact was stolen, which will now put the whole Doyle family in jeopardy."

Purnell shook his head. "The family are corrupt. Surely you can see that. Conrad's the sort of chap who needs to be managed. His late wife, I assume, held the finances together."

"And how do you know this?" I asked.

He simply looked at me and smiled. "I know many things. I also know that you are no detective, Ellen Tamar. Or do you prefer me to use the name your father granted, Lady Ellen?"

I pursed my lips. I was not fooled by his attempt to unnerve me. "I spent five long years treating men, many of whom took their last breath as I clutched their hands. I have little concern with frivolous etiquette and no time for your kind of privileged stance as if the suffering of others can be used for your own entertainment. You, sir, would do well to concentrate on good causes instead of gallivanting." I stared at him as he stopped. I saw a flash of something in his eyes. I knew I had got to him. Belittled him.

"I'm merely pointing out that you are not qualified to investigate a robbery and attempted murder," he said, the amusement now lost from his voice. "Granted, you were present during two murder investigations and I understand you were nearly killed just a couple of weeks ago. Whilst I admire such spirit from the weaker sex, you are no detective and could find yourself and your companion hurt."

"Is that a threat?" I said as my heart thumped. "And you include my companion? A young woman of seventeen?"

"I was not threatening you, I was gallantly warning you to take care," he said.

"I have Captain Hamilton to assist me with anything *you* may feel I'm not physically able to deal with," I said in a haughty voice.

"Do you really know the man?" he asked with his eyebrows raised.

"I attended to him some years ago, at Ashcombe Hall."

"But do you know his history, his family? Where it is they live?"

No, I did not, and I realised it had been rather remiss of me not to enquire after Hamilton's family. I knew his father was an accountant. But he had not spoken of them. I did not even know if both of his parents were still living.

"I didn't think so," Purnell said when I failed to answer his question. "So, you're not as close as I thought." He gave me another unnerving smile.

"I'm not baited by you Lord Purnell. Now, if you'd

care to leave me in peace, I need to gather my thoughts."

He laughed. "If you so wish, I will leave the great detective to contemplate."

I watched as he left the room and I knew there was something off about the man. If he was so intelligent, why did he get the day of the auction wrong? He clearly turned up early on purpose, maybe to get to the amulet before it was sold. He was a man with a plan and I intended to find out what that plan was.

After he left the room, Freddie swept in, her dress swishing around her. "Well, I never," she said, looking me up and down and fanning herself.

I frowned at her.

"I've never seen such attraction between a pair. Like fire." Her eyes danced as she picked her shawl up from the settee. "I've been listening from the passageway."

I could not find the words to comment.

She wrapped her shawl around her. "That man wants you and, looking at you now, I'd say the attraction is mutual."

"That's ridiculous," I said a little too loudly.

"This has made my mind up," she said, running her hand over the long hair which draped over her left shoulder. "I'll have no hope with Purnell with you here. I'll focus on Ernie." She turned around and left.

I slumped onto the settee. The trip to Moor House was becoming worse with every hour that passed. I remained seated alone for some minutes, calming myself.

"Ellen."

I looked up to find Lottie entering the drawing room.

I held out my hand and she took it and joined me on the settee. The sun had found its way through the clouds and streamed through the large bay window.

"I rather wish we had not come," I said, attempting to fight off the tears that threatened my eyes.

"I've just seen Freddie running down the garden, calling out for Ernest. Have you heard her calling him 'Ernie' all the time?"

"Captain Hamilton and I are not courting, he is free to seek whatever female company he wishes. I think you've allowed yourself to be carried away by your romantic nature." I smiled at her. "I know you hold much affection for us both."

She nodded. "I do, you've both made a difference to my life. But don't worry, he's never going to like her as much as he likes you."

I shook my head. "At this moment, I feel as if I simply want to return home to Ashcombe Hall as soon as possible. Life was busy there, it was harrowing to deal with some of the patients, but I felt strong and sure of myself, even when I lost Leonard. It gave me extra strength to help with the war. But now, I'm feeble and without purpose. Of course, I'm so pleased I have you and Prince with me. You're the only reason I'm glad I took the break away from the hall."

"Ellen, you've had a great time. You said so yourself. Don't let Freddie Doyle upset you like that."

"It's not her, it's the incorrigible Lord Purnell. He has mocked me. And Freddie accused me of having an attraction for the man." I sighed. "I simply want a peaceful time. Is it too much to ask for? Everywhere I go I find trouble."

"Ellen, please don't say that. You've brought families together, prevented people being wrongly sent to the gallows and saved them from wrongful imprisonment. I don't know what that Purnell man said to you, but he's probably jealous, one of those men who thinks women should be there to serve and have children."

I laughed. "Lottie, you speak much sense. You're a truly remarkable young woman. Here I am, wallowing in self-pity when you have been so strong."

She rubbed my hand. "I came to tell you that Ivy Wood is back in the kitchen and we have salmon for dinner. Why don't you come to the kitchen with me and we can speed the meal up. There's peeling to be done."

I smiled and stood up. I did so like spending time in the kitchen with my staff at Ashcombe Hall. I always found the kitchen a calming place, even when it was a hive of activity.

Chapter Ten

We walked down the slim passageway which was so unlike the wide corridors of Ashcombe Hall. It was dimly lit, even though it was daytime. This house had a distinct eerie feel as we passed portraits of the Victorian era which adorned the walls, as if the eyes of the painted people from years gone by were watching us. The house felt as if it had not been touched by the modern hand, even if its occupants were themselves thoroughly modern. I guessed that the late Mrs Doyle had been keen to preserve her family home and that Conrad Doyle had no wish to change it either. Beneath our feet were Turkish-style runners which were well-worn, from years of being trodden by many pairs of boots. We passed a room with a dark wooden closed door.

"That's Conrad's study," Lottie said, gesturing at it.

"I know, I've been in there myself," I said.

"I heard him in there with his son, just before that thing was stolen."

I looked at her and raised my eyebrows. "What were they saying?" I asked, realising that gave Robert Doyle an alibi. Then told myself off. Whilst I'd been asked to investigate, after the disagreeable interaction with Lord Purnell, I intended to distance myself until I could leave and relay everything that had happened to the police.

"Hmm, well his son was speaking in a low voice which was tricky to hear, but I did hear him say, 'Father, we have to tell the others.' And Mr Doyle replied in a louder voice. 'No, never!' – he was quite forceful."

"So, it appears that Robert and Conrad share a secret?" I said, wondering what that was. "But both have an alibi."

"Yes. I'll have to see if I can find some paper so I can make notes for you."

I shook my head and sighed. "I really do not want to become embroiled in this investigation. No note-taking is required."

"I don't blame you," Lottie said as we neared the kitchen. "I want to leave soon as well. I think that Conrad Doyle is snooty."

"It's likely a deflection to hide his own humble

upbringing," I said. "The nouveau riche are often the biggest of snobs."

We entered the kitchen and, without the earlier drama of a blood-covered Ivy Wood, I was able to take in the feel of the room. It was a bright space which looked onto the garden, with a large stove above which copper pots and a variety of utensils hung from hooks.

Ivy Wood sat at the table, preparing the fish.

"Would you care for any help?" I asked, looking at a pile of carrots.

"Mr Doyle would be angry if he thought I'd asked guests to prepare the meal," she said.

"I love preparing vegetables," I said. "It calms my nerves."

She filleted a large salmon, placing portioned sections into a large oven dish. "I know just what you mean and it's certainly helping me."

"How do you wish the carrots to be prepared?" I asked. "Into sticks julienne style?"

"Yes please, my lady. It would be most helpful, considering Grace sloped off with Robert when he was done with his father." She appeared much friendlier to me than when I first arrived and gave me a smile, showing her bright teeth.

"I'll scrub the potatoes," Lottie said, looking at the pile of small new potatoes. My mouth watered at the thought of them being doused with butter and paired with the oven baked fish.

I decided to commence the conversation with a less contentious issue. "I hope the weather cheers up, it's been awfully nice before today."

"I welcome the rain," Ivy said. "I hate too much heat. Although, maybe not this much rain. I've never seen anything like it!"

"Me neither." Now that I had opened her up, I decided to steer the conversation. "How was Mr Shaw when you checked on him?" I asked.

"He was relieved that you were here, my lady, and able to dress the wound. With all that blood and us being cut off from the rest of the world, poor Sid must have worried he would bleed to death." She turned to me. "I'm sure he would like to give his thanks to you. Being a trained nurse you surely saved his life."

I smiled, understanding that Ivy had respected my skills. Maybe prior to that she thought me an empty rich and entitled woman. "I will pop in and see him after we've eaten. I will change his dressing, to keep the wound as clean as possible."

"He's talking about going home, but I think he really should stay here. He lives in a small cottage, just before the bridge."

"There's another house?" I asked. I had not noticed it on the drive in.

"Yes, it was offered to me some years back, when Bert, the old gardener died. But I felt safer here in the house, so Shaw took it. Joseph couldn't have it then, he was only fifteen."

"Do you think The Magpie could be hiding in there?" Lottie asked her.

Ivy looked up from her work. "I assume Captain Hamilton is checking it with Joseph." She shook her head. "Conrad's desperate to get the thing back and he isn't thinking straight. None of us would do a thing like that. It was The Magpie, for sure, and he'll be long gone!"

"How's Joseph?" I asked. "He appeared quiet earlier on in the drawing room."

Mrs Wood gave an affectionate smile. "He always was a quiet lad and now he's a quiet man. Although twenty-four, he's mostly comfortable with his plants."

"It must have been nice for him to be brought up here," I said. "He's very loyal towards Mr Doyle."

"He knows nothing else, my lady. We're so lucky they took us in. A woman with a small child. There's no saying what would have happened to us, with my husband dead."

"Oh dear, how did he die?" I asked.

"He fell off a ladder in Exeter, where we lived at the time."

"I'm so sorry. I'm a widow too, but I can't imagine being left with a child," I said.

"Was Joseph upset at losing his father?" Lottie asked.

"I was pregnant when his father passed." Ivy sighed. "Joseph never knew him. I'll be forever in Winnie's debt. It was she who insisted we were given the job. A beautiful person she was. So kind to Joseph. He's close in age to Robert, only a few months between them. I guess that's what happened, she imagined herself in my position and took pity on me." She swallowed hard as if composing herself.

Grace entered the kitchen. "I'm going to make Robert a tea," she said. I noticed that her hair was a little dishevelled and her cheeks were flushed. Not in an extreme way, but enough for me to recognise a glow that I had not experienced myself since Leonard had died.

Ivy Wood tutted and stood up. She spoke in a low voice to Grace, but I overheard. "You need to watch yourself, you could end up with more than you bargained for. And he'll drop you like a hot stone if you..."

That confirmed my suspicion.

"I don't know what you're talking about," Grace hissed at Ivy as she moved across the kitchen and put the kettle on the stove.

Lottie looked at me confused and I decided to fill the awkward silence.

"How long have the Doyles owned this house?" I asked.

"Well, it was Mrs Doyle's family who owned it," Ivy said. "The Firths. The family built this house in 1856," she continued. "It only became the Doyle family home when Winnie's parents died."

"My father said Conrad only married Winnie Firth for the family money," Grace said. "Well, that and the fact he got her pregnant."

"Grace Thompson, do not speak ill of the dead." Ivy shook her head.

"My father said she was already showing when he wed them," she said indignantly.

"Your father may think he's high and mighty," Ivy said, "but just because he's the vicar don't make him a saint."

"What's that supposed to mean?" Grace said turning around.

"Your father's not got a good word to say about no one. And you need to watch your tongue, young lady." Ivy pointed her filleting knife at Grace. "Don't think I don't know what you're up to." She then pointed her knife upwards, to where the bedrooms were situated. "You're just trying to deflect attention from the pair of you."

Grace's face flushed crimson. "Robert was only born five months into the marriage. I heard that it was the talk of Dulverton at the time, even if folks don't say it to their faces. And Robert is well aware of what happened with his parents." She turned and gave Mrs Wood a coy look. "And you expect us to believe you had a husband before you came here."

Mrs Wood stood up. "That's enough."

Grace crossed her arms. "I don't know why you defend the family. Freddie inherited her father's ways, too, with how she carries on."

"You're a fine one to talk," Ivy said. "Only those without sin can cast the first stone." She sighed. "Mr Doyle was an artist and did not stick to the usual rules. I heard that he did wonders with a brush. It's a travesty he stopped painting when he came here."

"Your devotion is sweet, Ivy," Grace said. "I wonder if the next Mrs Doyle will be so welcoming to you?" She gave a short laugh.

As keen as I was to leave Moor House, this dose of gossip was drawing me in. Lottie sat beside me, wide-eyed.

Ivy went back to filleting her fish. "Mock me all you like, but if you've designs on being a Mrs Doyle you're deluded."

"Staff are often loyal to their employers," I said, feeling I needed to support Ivy under Grace's attack.

"My staff would defend me until the bitter end, whether or not I was guilty of something. Mrs Wood has lived here in this house for years. To her it will feel as if you're insulting her family. And you may wish to curb your criticism of the Doyles whilst under their roof."

Grace huffed but made no further comment as the kettle began to sing.

Lottie smiled at me, clearly enjoying the dressing down I had delivered.

"Thank you, my lady," Ivy Wood said in a small voice which told me I was continuing to win her over. "And thank you for preparing them carrots, they look perfect."

Whilst she had complimented me, I also took that to mean she would prefer to be left alone. I rather imagined she wanted to give Grace a proper dressing down without us witnessing it.

"Come along, Lottie," I said. "Let's leave Mrs Wood to her final preparations." I turned to Grace. "Is there anywhere in the house that myself and Lottie can freshen up?"

"There are two guest rooms with sinks upstairs, and I suppose you'll be staying the night," she said in a small voice, I guessed she was feeling the sting of my words. "I'll let Conrad know and then show you up." She followed us out of the kitchen with two cups of tea, probably realising that if she stayed she would have to endure Ivy's wrath.

After Grace had let Conrad know which room we would be using, we followed her up the dark, varnished wooden staircase to the upper level as she carried the cups. There were many rooms leading off the long landing.

"This one is ideal," she said, nodding at a door with 'Lavender Room' written upon it. "Freddie's room is opposite, if you need her. And Captain Hamilton's is the one next to that."

"Thank you," I said in a curt voice, telling myself not to be alarmed that Hamilton was spending the nights in a bedroom next to Freddie Doyle. After all this was not a huge hall, with separate wings – it was a family home.

We went inside. Grace left and we shut the door behind us. We heard a squeal and Lottie opened the door again and looked into the corridor.

"I thought I heard your voice," a male said.

"I'll spill the drinks," Grace said with a giggle.

We heard a door slam.

Lottie slowly closed our bedroom door and then turned around to face me, red-faced. "Grace's been dragged into a room by Robert Doyle, and she did not protest!" she hissed.

"That's what Mrs Wood was speaking to her about."

"Oh, I get it now." She shook her head. "They're a couple?"

"Not officially, but yes, it would seem they are exceptionally well acquainted." I gestured to the sink, wondering whether I had struck a nerve with regard to Lottie and Sebastian. "Come along, let's have a wash," I said changing the subject before Lottie could dwell on her own situation. "We can chat about this theft." I had no intention of investigating but knew that when Lottie's mind rested, she was often consumed by her broken heart. "Who do you think stole the amulet?" I asked her.

"The Magpie," Lottie said. "Not that I know what an amulet is!"

"It's a good luck charm. But I've no idea what this one looks like as Conrad has been secretive about it."

"It didn't bring much luck to Mr Shaw, did it?" Lottie said. "The Magpie is probably somewhere in the woods soaked through. He could have walked for miles on the moor. He could be back home, having hidden the amulet, and eating dinner with his wife, as if nothing has happened."

"But if it was not The Magpie and someone in this house, who would you think it was?" I asked, interested to see what her gut feelings told her, as I could not make sense of it myself.

"I don't really like any of them," she said. "Any of them lot could have done it."

"Even Joseph?"

"He sat there all quiet and didn't say much, did he? He might be hiding something. But it can't have been Robert or Conrad Doyle, I heard them not long before I heard Ivy screaming."

"Even without an alibi, Conrad Doyle would have no reason to steal his own item. I don't think Robert would have anything to gain either, by taking from his own father, the man who is supporting him, when he is supposed to be taking over the family business. Where were you at the time of the theft?"

"I was on my way up to the lavatory, having just overheard Conrad in his study."

"Once we've spoken to Mr Shaw, we may be able to ascertain whether the thief left via the window and roof, or whether he escaped through the house."

"I don't like that Freddie," Lottie said. "I don't trust her one bit. And she was rude to us."

"She's a little brash, I give you that, but she's an independent woman, living in a commune in London, and has a simple life," I said. "I'm not sure she would even be bothered by an amulet and she certainly would not want to live off any money generated by her father. She has a clear disdain for him."

"She could have could taken the amulet to hurt him and her brother," Lottie said. "And she's too interested in Ernest," Lottie said.

I laughed. "You may wish it to be her for that reason."

"And I'm not sure about that Lord Purnell, neither," she said.

"He's certainly enjoying himself too much," I added. "Most inappropriate. A man who enjoys conflict. Someone who gains pleasure out of disrupting a situation. He's probably too rich for his own good, not knowing what to do with himself, and thoroughly bored so he's entertaining himself by being extremely annoying."

"The way he was looking at you, Ellen," Lottie said. "I didn't want to mention it earlier as you were upset. But I think he likes you."

"Freddie is a willing companion, should he wish for female company over the next day or so. She was positively salivating over him." I wished Purnell would divert his attention to her.

"Who else is there?" Lottie asked, her mood seeming to have lightened.

"Grace. She lost her job here, she probably wants a life with Robert, which will not receive the blessing of

Conrad Doyle. I'm guessing he will encourage his son to also find a wealthy wife." I sighed. "The amulet is likely to be quite small."

"It'll be like finding a needle in a haystack," Lottie said.

"The house has many rooms. And it would not be worth us looking for something when we have no idea what it looks like," I said.

"That Lord Purnell has seen it. I bet he would tell you what it looks like if you asked him nicely," Lottie said with a laugh.

"Hamilton has seen it, I would prefer to ask him," I said. "But I think the best thing that can happen is for the bridge to be fixed in a speedy fashion so we can leave."

We washed in thoughtful silence and combed our hair into shape, adding a little pomade and then rouge to our cheeks. Although I did not add much to mine, since I appeared to blush quite frequently with the disagreeable Lord Purnell in the house.

There was a knock at the door.

"Hello?" I called out.

"Ellen, Lottie, it's me," Hamilton called. "I have Prince."

I glanced in the dressing table mirror and stood up, smoothing down my pale blue dress. "Come in," I said.

Hamilton appeared flustered as he opened the

door. "Sorry for my appearance," he said as Prince lolloped in and lay in front of the fireplace. "I've spent nearly an hour on the grounds. I'm off to my room, but letting you know in case I am late to dinner, and I wanted to apologise again. I have put you in a most awful position and now you are stuck here."

He stared into my eyes. Before me was the Hamilton I had grown fond of even if, as Purnell had pointed out, I knew little of the man's personal life. I decided that I would get to know more about him during the next day or so, about his family, about his life, whilst the bridge was being mended – and then we could finally leave for Denham Hall.

Chapter Eleven

In the dining room, our starter consisted of a colourful salad, prepared using vegetables and herbs from the kitchen garden. Following this, Ivy brought the steaming fish, potatoes and vegetables which she had placed on the hostess trolley.

"The meal smells divine, Mrs Wood," I said.

She smiled at me and I noticed the Doyles taking it all in their stride as they practically shovelled the food onto their plates with little sense of gratitude. *Such a disagreeable family,* I thought.

"I agree, it looks lovely," Lottie added from my side.

Freddie was opposite me with Lord Purnell to her left. Conrad appeared to have abandoned his quest to make me his bride and was sitting at the head of the table, speaking in a low voice to his son who sat to his right.

"If you're all happy," Ivy said. "I'm taking Shaw his meal so will be at his bedside should you need me." She turned to Robert with pursed lips. "Grace is in the kitchen, should you require anything."

"She's no longer our employee," Robert said from his father's side.

"She's still in the kitchen though, isn't she?" Ivy swept away before Robert could reply, clearly with undertones that Grace was good enough for him to spend time alone with, yet not good enough for the Doyle dining table.

Lottie did not even look up and kept her eyes on her food. I knew she felt far from comfortable at the Doyle dining table.

Freddie laughed. "She used to be so quiet, so meek. She's certainly come out of her shell since Mother died. Next she'll be sitting opposite you Father, at this very table."

Conrad gave his daughter a warning glare and a silence followed. This was broken shortly afterwards when Hamilton entered the room and took the seat to the right of Freddie and smiled across the table at me and then dished himself the food.

I turned to Hamilton. "Have you managed to visit your family at all recently?"

He smiled. "I have not, but I write to them and

they love to hear of you, Ellen. I will visit them before my next contract begins."

"Do invite them to the hall once I return," I said with a smile.

"That would be really nice," Lottie said. "I would love to meet them."

"I'm sure they will find you excellent company, Lottie," Hamilton said. "And Ellen, it is so generous of you, they would love that. I often speak of how beautiful the gardens are. Father loves his roses and you have such fine specimens, if I remember correctly?"

I gave Purnell a smug look before turning back to Hamilton. "Of course, they are the pride and joy of my gardener."

"How super," Purnell said. "Captain. Tell me, how did you find your time in the war?"

Hamilton poured himself a glass of wine. "It was a destructive time where many men lost their lives. I've moved on. And yourself?"

"I was unable to enlist," Purnell said.

I laughed. "If that is the case, Lord Purnell, that you were too young, you have not aged at all well."

He threw his head back and laughed. "I admire your keen sense of humour." He turned to Hamilton. "I extended my studies."

"So you were excused out of privilege?" I asked.

"There's nothing wrong with being a conscientious objector," Freddie said. "I admire that in a man."

Purnell rubbed the side of his nose. "I was completing a research paper abroad. I was unable to return due to the hostilities, it was not possible for me to travel. It was important work."

Hamilton raised his eyebrows as if he did not believe Purnell but, whilst he had much to criticise the man for, he left it at that. Hamilton, being a gentleman, did not court conflict as Purnell did. It all sounded rather vague to me. I pondered the notion of asking Purnell about his research paper but assumed it would be lies and how could I question it? It would no doubt be a subject I knew nothing of. I also did not want him to think I was remotely interested in his history. I turned to Conrad who had now ended his conversation with his son and begun eating his meal.

"Mr Doyle, I'm sure your amulet was most beautiful. Do you have any knowledge of where it originated? And it would help if you could please describe the piece."

He took a deep breath. "I have to accept that I'm unlikely to see it again. It was from a pharaoh's tomb."

"Grave theft, I knew it," Freddie said, sitting back in her seat.

Conrad ignored his daughter. "It was crafted from

polished black basalt, a commonly used material in ancient Egyptian art and artefacts."

"Basalt holds symbolic significance," Robert added. "It represents the fertile and life-giving black soil left behind by the annual flooding of the River Nile. It emphasises its connection to the cycle of life, death and rebirth, central to ancient Egyptian beliefs."

"Well done, big brother," Freddie said. "It appears you learned something at university after all!"

Robert shut his eyes for a second and inhaled, then reopened them and continued. "I will be travelling to Egypt in November with my old university professor."

"To rob more graves," Freddie added before returning to her meal.

"The piece was certainly captivating," Purnell said. "The intricate hieroglyphics and carvings were most beautiful. Such a shame it's now lost. If it was this Magpie chap you talk of, he's probably ignorant of the true value and it will disappear."

"Amulets have spiritual significance. It's an excellent piece for any collection," Robert added. "A highly sought-after treasure for collectors and historians alike. And yes, it is likely now to be lost, but I'm sure the person that has it is not a petty thief."

"It's gone, forever," Conrad said before taking a large mouthful of wine.

"How big was the piece?" I asked.

"Three inches, I'd say," Hamilton said. "Easy to conceal."

"It's a shame the world will not see it," I said.

"They wouldn't have anyway, it was clearly destined for a private collection," Freddie said.

Conrad took another large mouthful of wine. "There are enough artefacts making their way to the British Museum for the public to see."

"When I'm next in London, I will have to visit the British Museum," I said.

"An excellent idea, I would love to accompany you," Lord Purnell said.

I paused but made no comment. I knew the man enjoyed every interaction he had with me. But why? I certainly did not know.

"If you're in town, be sure to look *me* up," Freddie said to Purnell.

Purnell looked amused as he lifted his wine glass to his mouth. In the distance, I heard a bark.

Lottie wiped her mouth on her napkin and then moved her chair away from the table and stood up. "Excuse me. I'll check on Prince." She left and I felt the relief she felt at her escape.

I attempted to enjoy my meal as Freddie asked Hamilton questions about his family. I noted that she had asked more questions in ten minutes than I had in many weeks. I learned that they lived in a small but pretty house which used to be the vicarage in a small village outside Bath. Hamilton's grandfather had been the local vicar, but the church closed during the war as there was another in the neighbouring village. His mother was a keen baker and he had an older sister who had children. As I ate, I felt rather glum that Freddie had discovered all of this information. And as Hamilton spoke of his family, he became increasingly animated. I had to admit that it was Freddie who had put the smile upon his face – not me.

I dabbed my mouth with a napkin. "If you will excuse me, I will relieve Mrs Wood from sitting with Mr Shaw. I need to attend to him." I wanted to refresh his dressing and ensure there was no sign of infection.

The gentlemen stood as I rose from the table and Freddie shook her head slowly. I hurried down the corridor once I was outside the room, as I wished to locate Lottie. She was in the scullery with Prince, he had emptied his food bowl and was now chomping on the large bone we had brought with us from Phoebe's kitchens. He stood up and approached me, wagging his tale and whining. I knew he wanted a walk.

"I'm off to see Mr Shaw, will you come with me, Lottie?"

"Of course." She stood up.

I stroked Prince's head. "Sorry, boy. Be good and stay here and then we will take you for a run in the gardens." I looked out of the small scullery window to see the clouds were dispersing.

As we entered the room, Ivy stood up. "Sid's feeling much better, aren't you, dear?" she said to him. I guessed they were like family, as were my staff back at Ashcombe Hall.

He nodded at me and blinked nervously. "I've failed Mr Doyle."

"Nonsense, he put you in a vulnerable position, guarding what appears to be a priceless piece which should really be sold within an establishment like Sotherby's, with adequate security." I paused. "Not that Captain Hamilton is not capable, but one man cannot keep eyes on a property with such a large and unmanageable boundary. Indeed, Mr Doyle has put both yourself and Captain Hamilton in great danger."

Shaw lowered his head.

"Lady Ellen is right," Ivy said. "As much as we want to be of help to Conrad, he probably regrets not selling it elsewhere." Ivy gestured at Shaw. "I'll make you some more sweet tea." She picked up his empty plate and left the room.

I smiled at Mr Shaw. "I need to change the dressing to keep it as clean as possible before the doctor can reach you."

"Thank you, my lady," he said, then gave Lottie a weak smile.

Lottie stood up, went to the window and looked outside, as if to give him some privacy, then chattered away about the rain and how heavy it had been whilst I redid his dressing. I could tell Shaw felt uncomfortable with the situation, so I worked as quickly as possible. It had been some time since I had dressed and redressed wounds but it was something I did with ease.

"There we are, all done," I said with a smile.

He sighed and laid himself back on the pillow. "I'm never the best patient."

I laughed. "I've experienced every type of patient." I took the chair which Ivy had been seated on. Lottie turned around and lowered herself onto the window seat.

"I thought I was a goner there. There's much I haven't yet done." He winced. "I'm thirty-five and have no wife. No child."

I blinked, thinking of Leonard. His life was much shorter and certainly different to Shaw's, yet real human needs transcend class.

"Do you have a sweetheart?" I asked him.

"No. But I have known love for a woman." He trailed off.

"Life has more meaning when you have someone you would move mountains for," I said.

He shook his head. "I wasn't strong enough. That's

my problem. Didn't have much to offer. I'm a weak man. Look at me."

I wondered whether he meant he was not strong enough to fight for the woman he had loved or not strong enough to overpower the thief. "You were attacked with a knife. You were unarmed. There is no shame in that. Is there anything you can tell us about your attacker?" I asked. "Conrad wishes me to investigate the matter for him."

"You're a detective?" he asked.

"Not really, but I have solved a couple of murders recently."

"Murder?" He looked panicked.

"I'm keen to leave this matter to the police, although I understand Mr Doyle wishes them to be kept in the dark. But you have been stabbed, we don't want another person hurt, do we?"

He shook his head and I saw him visibly gulp.

"As we're marooned here, I'm doing as Conrad wishes and looking into the matter until the bridge is cleared and I can leave. Can you describe to me how the attacker looked?"

"He was dressed in black, my lady."

"Height, build? Did he say anything? Did he have any strong aftershave or smell of a particular brand of soap?"

"Just dressed in black," he said meekly.

"Was he tall or short?" Lottie asked.

He frowned and I had no idea why Shaw was avoiding answering the questions.

"Where did the man come from?" I asked. "From the door to the room, or in through the window?"

"I looked up and he was there." Shaw looked down at his hands. "Please don't tell Mr Doyle, but I have to confess."

"To what?" I asked.

He looked at me sheepishly. "It was so warm up there and in that comfortable chair, I was overcome with tiredness and I drifted off to sleep." He shook his head. "Conrad's been having me guard the piece around the clock as Captain Hamilton checks the perimeter. The Magpie could have come in the through the door or the window."

"So you were sleeping when he arrived? Tell me what you saw when you awoke?" I asked.

"I woke up to find I was on the floor and my side hurt. I looked up but my vision was blurred and I saw a figure in black facing away from me. I called out. Then I passed out. So I didn't see how they came in or how they left. But Ivy said to me earlier that he was gone by the time she got there." He sighed. "I've really let Mr Doyle down."

"It's his own fault for working you so hard," Lottie said.

"So all you saw was that they were dressed in black?" I asked.

He nodded. "It was so hot up there, I opened the window. On the top floor there's hardly any air. I was glad of the shower, it cooled everything down so it was a lovely temperature. I drifted off to the sound of the rain."

"Well, it certainly appears he left by the fire rope," I said. "It had your blood on it."

"I hate seeing blood," he said. "Next thing I know you're there, asking me how I'm feeling, but I couldn't wake up properly."

"You murmured that it was The Magpie then fainted." I frowned at him. "Maybe you were concussed, from your fall to the floor." I checked his head. "I can't see a bump." I sat back in my seat.

"Are you sure it was a man?" Lottie asked.

Shaw paused. "All I can see in my mind is a flash of someone dressed in black, as I already said, they were facing away. I saw no eyes. I think they wore a tight woollen hat. Again, black. It all happened so quick. It's just a blur."

"That's very helpful," I said, although it could of course have been anyone. "Do you think it was the person they call The Magpie?"

"It must have been. I feel terrible for Mr Doyle, he said he's going to have to let me go if he doesn't find it. I live on the land too, in the cottage. I'll have to find other work. I'll lose my home without the job."

"I'm so sorry, Mr Shaw. If the item turns up then maybe things will resolve themselves," I said.

He shook his head. "He's angry with me, he'll probably let me go whatever happens." He glanced at me. "Thank you so much for everything you've done. You are an amazing woman, a nurse and someone who cares about everyone, not just the privileged."

"I'm sure Mr Doyle isn't angry with you," I said, brushing over the compliment.

"And we won't tell him you were asleep," Lottie said. "He doesn't need to know. We'll say the thief took you by surprise."

Mr Shaw stifled a yawn.

I stood up. "I'll leave you to sleep, but please do not worry and don't blame yourself, you have done absolutely nothing wrong."

After we left the room, I felt rather tired myself. "Let's take Prince for a walk and have an early night," I said to Lottie. I had no wish to spend the evening with the Doyle family. "We may see things in a fresh light in the morning."

Chapter Twelve

It was early morning and lay on my side in the single bed. In my eyeline was Lottie, still sleeping for it was only six o'clock. As well as twin beds, the room contained a dressing table, hand basin and a dark, polished wardrobe. Beyond Lottie was a window facing out to the front of the house, and I could see the foliage from the trees which was mostly obscured by the dresses we had worn the previous day hanging and moving slightly in the gentle breeze. We had requested soap flakes before we retired and had wiped down our dresses with a washcloth. With the morning sunshine, I expected them to be dry. We had washed our undergarments, even though we had spare for the current day, as we did not know how long we would be marooned at Moor House. At least we would feel relatively fresh after having bathed in a large bath in the neighbouring room. The house was rather pleasant and under different circumstances, I would have enjoyed staying there. To spend time in a more intimate residence than Ashcombe Hall.

I sat up, wearing a nightdress which had belonged to the late Mrs Doyle. Now fully awake, I rose quietly from the bed and Prince padded over from where he had been in slumber. Once dressed, I tiptoed from the room, leaving Lottie to sleep. I took Prince with me as I wanted to ensure he had a comfort break.

Downstairs, I entered the kitchen and found Grace lifting the boiling kettle from the stove, no doubt fetching Robert a drink.

"Good morning, my lady," she said. "I see you too are an early riser."

I nodded. "I need to take Prince outside for a run."

"He's such a lovely dog," she said. "You can tell how much he loves you. And loves life."

I smiled as Prince ran to the door. "I'll let him have a wander outside," I said as I opened the door for him. I knew he would not travel too far from me. I wished to take this opportunity to ask Grace a few questions about the Doyles.

"Would you like some tea, my lady?" she asked and lifted the pot.

"Yes please," I said as I sat down. "I gather you're rather close to Robert Doyle?"

She sighed. "We always got on well when I worked here, and I comforted him when his mother died. We used to hide up in the attic room whilst Conrad entertained all sorts of people in this house." She shook her head. "Robert was so upset with him and Freddie had left so he had no one to confide in. Then when Conrad ran into financial difficulty, he said he could not afford to pay me any more. Although I think it was because I was close to Robert." She poured the teas. "Robert missed me and started visiting me at the inn."

"You're courting?" I asked.

"Yes, but Mr Doyle does not approve. Even though my father is the vicar, I'm not good enough for his family. It's a cheek considering he comes from a lower place than me. I'm still treated like staff whenever I'm here." She passed me a filled tea cup. "And as you can imagine, with Conrad's parties, my father does not approve of me spending time with this family either! Father also hates me working at the inn, but I enjoy it. I serve in the bar and carry out the deliveries, which was the reason I was here yesterday, delivering wine for the guests Conrad was expecting to bid on the amulet. We won't be short of drinks whilst we're stuck here!"

"Do you think it's possible The Magpie got to hear of the artefact and stole it?"

She shook her head. "It's not The Magpie."

"Why do you say that?" I asked.

She lowered her voice. "Mark my words it's someone in this house. And it wasn't Robert."

"Where were you at the time of the crime?" I asked.

"In the barn checking on the horse." She took a sip of her tea. "That's why I'm up early, to check on him. He's old. I'll have to exercise him somehow. If he'd been a younger horse, they probably would have sent him away to war." She shook her head. "Brenton should really be put out to pasture, but you can't get good horses these days, most are still being broken in." She smiled. "That horse is the main reason I love my job."

I wanted to steer Grace back to the stolen amulet. "If you're sure it was someone in this house that stole the amulet, who do you think it was?"

"Freddie hates her father, maybe she wants to hurt him? And Ivy might appear to dote on Conrad, but I used to work here and she was unhappy a few times. He had her in tears. Robert thinks that when his mother died, Ivy expected his father to turn to her. But he didn't, he turned to the drink and wild parties." She took a deep breath. "But having said that, it's likely to be that stranger."

"Lord Purnell?" I asked.

"You called, my lady?"

I spun around to find Purnell grinning at us from the doorway.

"We were just debating who stole the artefact," I said to him.

"So I heard and I do believe I'm a suspect." He grinned at us.

Grace flushed pink, clearly realising he had overheard.

"But of course," I said. "We know nothing about you other than the fact that you liked the amulet and put a handsome bid on it. You are an obvious suspect."

"I can understand I may look guilty." He shrugged as he entered the room. "The stranger." He looked into my eyes.

I glanced away and took a sip of my tea. "How did you find out about the sale?"

"I could tell you," Purnell said as he walked into the room. "But it's confidential. Feel free to ask Conrad for the name of his agent." He shot a look at Grace. "Sleep well?"

She blushed. "Would you care for a tea, my Lord?"

"I shall have some water then take a brisk walk. Would you care to join me, Lady Ellen?"

I shook my head. "I'm taking tea up to Lottie. I'm here watching my dog. Take care if he approaches you."

"Thank you for the warning." Purnell poured

himself a glass of water, drank it and then went out to the gardens through the kitchen door.

I watched then flinched as Prince bounded up to him, hoping my dog would not snarl as he often did at people I disliked. But Purnell leaned down and gave Prince a scratch behind the ear, which my dog enjoyed. Then he rolled on the floor to have his tummy stroked. The man was a charmer indeed.

"I don't know what to make of him," Grace said as she put another kettle of water on the stove. "But I know I don't trust him."

"My thoughts exactly." We watched through the glass as he threw sticks for Prince.

I asked Grace about the church where she grew up to pass the time while she made more tea. She left the kitchen with two filled cups on a tray with some buttered bread, no doubt for herself and Robert to enjoy in his room.

I was only alone for a moment. By the time I had topped the tea pot up with water, Ivy entered the room.

"Ah, good morning, my lady. It's a fine day today, hopefully they'll fix the bridge and you can make your way back to Denham Hall," she said. "I'll be making soup for luncheon if you're still here. Joseph grows many vegetables in the kitchen garden."

"How lovely," I said. "I will have a wander over to

see your kitchen garden. It will remind me of home." I sighed. "It feels so long since I was at Ashcombe Hall." I poured a cup of tea to take up to Lottie and then glanced out to the garden. I planned to call Prince in but instead left him to his games with Purnell. I had no wish to spend any more time with the curious lord.

I made my way upstairs.

As Lottie drank her tea, I filled her in on what Grace had told me.

"Who are you going to interrogate next?" she asked.

"Joseph. If you come down with me we'll seek him out."

Chapter Thirteen

When we reached the kitchen, Ivy was preparing breakfast. We looked out to the gardens to see Purnell still throwing sticks for Prince.

"Do you mind collecting Prince for me?" I asked Lottie.

"You can't take him into the kitchen garden," Ivy said. "My Joseph won't want the chickens scared. There's never been any pets at Moor House. We've had stray cats come in but Conrad makes us catch them and release them away from here. Although Shaw has a black cat called Fly that he feeds down at the cottage."

"I see," I said.

"I'll ask Lord Purnell to mind Prince for us," Lottie

said. Then laughed as she saw my dog running after him. "Prince seems to like him."

"Lord Purnell is a charmer. Never trust a charmer," I warned her.

"Never a truer word said," Ivy added bitterly. "And there's something not quite right about that one."

I waited at the top of the garden for Lottie as she went to and from Purnell. He looked up at me as they chatted and waved. Considering he was minding Prince, I raised my hand in a thank you, but did not break into a smile. I knew I must interview the man but was putting that off. I certainly had no wish to do so alone. I felt he had undisclosed intentions.

Lottie returned beaming at me. "He's really funny," she said.

"I'm sure he is," I said, then pursed my lips.

Lottie looked back at him. "But I have to remember he's our top suspect."

We made our way across the garden to a gate set into a long stone wall which encased the kitchen garden. I pushed it open and we walked inside. It was beautifully tended, with neat rows of vegetables, herbs and lavender. Chickens clucked as they meandered around the plants. Ahead, Joseph was turning over soil. He stopped as we approached.

"Good morning, my lady," he said, leaning on the

handle of his spade. "And Miss Penny." He smiled bashfully at Lottie.

"Your mother was telling me about this garden. It's beautiful and bursting with vegetables. I understand you're providing the ingredients for a soup your mother plans to make?"

"Leek, potato and herbs," he said.

"My favourite," Lottie said.

"It certainly sounds delicious." I gestured around the garden, taking in the trellises up against the walls, bursting with plants full of fruits and many runner beans. "You seem to love it out here."

"I do. This is where I'm happiest." He stood tall and gestured around the garden. "I've nurtured every plant from a seedling."

"How did you learn?" Lottie asked.

"From the previous gardener. Old Bert taught me everything he knew, but he passed when I was just gone fifteen. Then as the years passed I had to grow vegetables not just for the house but also for the village, what with the war and things being tight."

"Mr Doyle is very proud of you," I said. "That I can tell."

Joseph beamed. It was so nice to see someone respecting Mr Doyle. Joseph clearly had a lot of regard for his employer.

"It's a shame someone has stolen from him," I said. "Did you see anything suspicious before Shaw was killed?"

"No."

"Where were you?" I asked casually.

"I was on my way over here when I heard Ma cry out. It's a disgusting thing to do to Sid," Joseph grumbled.

"Do you think it was The Magpie?" I asked.

"No one knew about it. Why would The Magpie come back here when he already stole Mrs Doyle's jewellery? How would he have even known about it?"

"Have you anyone particular in mind?" I asked.

"I wouldn't put it past his own children, they're ungrateful and have no respect for their father and what he's done for them," he said.

"Really? Freddie and Robert?"

He sighed. "Mr Doyle should have stuck with his artwork."

"Really?" Lottie said.

"Yes, he's a gifted man. A practical man. Some people are meant to work with their hands. He was forced to marry and give up his passions."

Hmm, I thought, remembering Grace saying that Robert had been conceived well before his parents' wedding. I guessed Winnie's father had forced Conrad to marry his daughter.

Joseph dug the soil. "That won't ever happen to me. Mr Doyle's life would have been different if he'd stuck with his dreams. Giving up art has left him empty, looking elsewhere for happiness, false happiness. He needs to get back to his art. That's all." He stood up and looked around at the vegetables. "If I had to give all of this up, I'd be a broken man."

"Why do you think it could be Freddie or Robert?" I asked.

"Freddie is always saying she hates the way her father has acted since her mother died. I think she blames him for her death in some way."

"And what do you think of Lord Purnell?" I asked.

He shrugged. "Seems like a nice man. I don't think he'd have done it. He's rich. Why steal?"

He'd made a good point and I had no intention of asking him whether his mother should be in the frame. Prince barked and I turned to see him pressing his snout through the railings of the gate.

"I'd better get back to my dog," I said.

"He seems nice," Lottie said as we walked away. "He's got no motive and it's not going to be good for him if Conrad has to sell."

"I agree."

As we left the kitchen garden, Prince jumped excitedly around our legs. Purnell waved at us then disappeared into the woods at the end of the garden.

"I wonder where he's off to?" I said.

"Shall we follow him?" Lottie asked.

"No!" I said quickly, then turned to see Conrad Doyle standing on the kitchen doorstep.

He waved at me.

"I'm returning to the house," I said. "I need to speak with Conrad. Will you be fine out here with Prince?"

"Yes." She looked towards the woods.

"And don't follow Purnell, you should avoid being alone with him." I could read her easily, and I was sure she'd intended to follow him into the wooded area.

As I reached the kitchen door, Conrad gave me a weak smile.

"I would be grateful if you would accompany me to my study," he said. "I've heard that you've been interviewing everyone. It's much appreciated. I'd love to hear what you've learned so far. You really are my only hope." He gestured outside. "Captain Hamilton's doing a thorough search of the entire periphery for any clues or evidence that someone has broken through."

I followed Conrad through the kitchen and past Ivy, who nodded at me. When we reached the study, we both took seats and I sat opposite him as he perched his elbows on the desk and looked at me intently.

"So what have you deduced so far?" he asked with

so much hope in his eyes it made me feel guilty for wanting to flee as soon as the bridge was fixed.

"At the top of the list, we have Lord Purnell, a mysterious figure who no one knows. He's clearly an intelligent man, why would he make an error with the date of his appointment? What do you know about him?" I asked.

"Nothing at all, I've yet to pick up the final list of bidders which the agent had set up. I know no more about him than you do, other than that he's a rich man, has an expensive car and has made me a handsome offer for the amulet."

"You were not given his name before he arrived?"

"No, and I need to get to town so that I can telegram the agent and ask him to cancel the rest of the visitors."

"So the agent would have contacted Purnell direct?" I began to feel even more suspicious as far as Purnell was concerned. "What was your conversation with the fellow when he arrived?"

"Firstly, I admired his car. Then I asked if he was here for the auction and he said yes, he was."

"You mentioned the auction before he did?" I asked.

"I did, yes. Then I asked whether Cuthbert of Jessops had sent him, and he confirmed he had."

Oh dear, I thought. Conrad clearly had not vetted Purnell in an appropriate manner.

"And he put in a large bid." He sighed and shook his head. "I need that amulet back. I've one bidder, I don't need anyone else to turn up. I just need that amulet. I'll be more than happy with what Purnell offered, it will see me right for years." He looked up at me. "So what else have you deduced?"

"I understand someone dressed in black came at Mr Shaw with a knife, stabbed him, stole the amulet and made off out of the window. But we cannot be one hundred percent certain as Shaw fell unconscious. It appears he has an aversion to the sight of blood."

"You think it's likely to be The Magpie, then?" Conrad asked with a sigh.

"If it was this Magpie character, he's extremely agile, scaling roofs, crawling inside small spaces. It would not take much for such a man to climb a few trees to escape your property. Even if he took the steep bank and made his way alongside the river. It would be easy terrain for someone used to such acrobatic feats."

"Do you think it really is him and any search will be fruitless?"

"I would...except..." I paused.

Conrad leaned forward. "Go on."

I looked at him thoughtfully. "Has The Magpie stabbed any of his victims before?"

Conrad frowned. "Not that I know of."

"In that case, I would be loathe to accept it was him. From what you've told me, the theft of the amulet does not sound as if it was carried out by the same person. A jewel thief who strikes in the night, who has until now hurt no one. This was daylight robbery of an Egyptian artefact, which would not be easily sold on without specific knowledge and contacts."

Conrad looked a little cheered. "If it is a person within the house, maybe the amulet's still here...somewhere." He leaned back in his seat.

"Indeed. And if you had to point the finger at anyone yourself?" I asked. "Who would it be?"

He ran a hand over his hair. "In my mind I've blamed everyone, even my own flesh and blood. I've not been the best father. And I've not certainly not been the best employer."

I rose from the chair. "I'll continue to ask questions. But if you will excuse me," I said. "I need to check on my dog." I also wished to check on the progress of the bridge.

As if reading my mind, Conrad gestured out of the window. "I hear they've started moving the tree. Robert went down to the bridge, to take a look. There's a group of men cutting the fir into pieces so that it's manageable to remove. We're fortunate that it wasn't a much heavier tree, otherwise the bridge would have fallen in.

Thank you for your help," he said with what appeared to be a genuine smile. "If the amulet doesn't turn up, I've some tough decisions to make.

"If it is not recovered, would you be able to take up painting again?" I asked softly.

He shook his head. "I've lost my gift."

In that moment, I felt sorry for the man.

Having left the study, I exited the house via the front entrance and strolled around the periphery. The sun shone and I appreciated that it was indeed a beautiful property. Vines climbed up the stone walls in places and many bushes bursting with colour held tweeting birds. As I rounded the property, Hamilton strode towards me with his stick over his arm. As I observed him, I wished I'd never suggested he carry a stick until his night terrors subsided. Six years had since passed, and the man still used it. I'd spoken to him a few weeks previously and it appeared that he continued to have the odd bad dream. I decided it was high time he let it go.

"Ellen, how are you this morning?" he asked with a smile.

"The sunshine helps. I was planning to take a stroll to see how the mending of the bridge was coming along," I said. "Would you care to join me?"

"That's an excellent idea. It will be good to get

away from the house. I have carried out a final check and can find no evidence that there was an intruder. And with no artefact to guard, I'm free to accompany you."

"I will let Lottie know," I said.

Chapter Fourteen

Lottie declined to join us on our walk to the bridge, which I guessed was because she was hoping that with Hamilton and I alone, something romantic would develop. I left Prince with her considering someone had been stabbed at the property.

We strolled down the slope of the back garden.

"There's a shortcut this way," Hamilton said. "The gate is locked, but I have the key." He pulled a large set of keys from his pocket.

"This house has many locked doors by the looks of it," I said, wondering which room held Conrad's artwork, and whether Hamilton held the key to it, as I was curious to see his art and whether it was a good standard.

As we reached the woods, Purnell was heading

back to the house. He nodded at us with a smile as he passed.

"What do you make of him?" I whispered to Hamilton.

"I don't trust the man," he said.

"And neither do I." I looked over my shoulder as Purnell headed for the house. "Conrad had not even heard of him before yesterday. No one knows who that man is and he may be pretending that he was here for the auction." I recounted to Hamilton the information I had extracted from Conrad.

"Anyone interested in purchasing an Egyptian artefact under circumstances steeped in such secrecy is surely a crook," Hamilton said. "He may have heard about the amulet via another source."

"Exactly, Conrad is probably going to encourage the man to stay, hoping the amulet shows up – Lord Purnell apparently offered him a tidy sum for it."

"It was supposed to be a silent auction," Hamilton said, "But Purnell blurted an amount out whilst Shaw and I were there. It was exceedingly high."

"It would not surprise me if the fellow was stringing Mr Doyle along."

"I agree. These excessively rich people with no purpose clearly have to make up their own forms of entertainment."

I had deduced the same, but then fell silent. I was,

you could say, excessively rich myself. Although I'd previously had purpose, running the convalescent home, now I had no purpose at all. I stopped in my tracks. "Do you think that's why I'm embroiling myself in these mysteries. Because I have no purpose? That I'm attracted to the thrill of it because I've an easy life?"

Hamilton turned to me. "Ellen, I am sorry, that was not meant to be a slight against your character."

I continued walking. "But I have no purpose, I could be looking for trouble to make my life more interesting."

"You've been far from living for pure entertainment like Lord Purnell would appear to. And he skipped the war. You've been helping others, that is your nature. To help other people. It drives you to find the truth."

"You make me sound so virtuous," I said with a laugh.

We reached the river and took a stroll along the bank, away from the bridge. We stopped at the water's edge.

"You're an amazing woman," Hamilton said as the river, full to the brim, moved quickly towards Dulverton.

I turned to look at him. "Thank you, Ernest." In that moment, I felt so close to him, as if I wanted to reach out. The air between us became thick and for one fearful moment I thought he was going to embrace me. As much as I'd dreamed of it, I was far too shy for that, especially in broad daylight. In an effort to escape the situation, I mindlessly snatched his stick, pulled my arm back and launched it into the river.

He stood aghast as the stick, his crutch for six years, splashed into the water and was carried along in the torrent towards town.

I put my hand up to my mouth, as if I'd only just realised what I'd done. I swallowed, waiting for a reaction.

Hamilton laughed. "I guess it was about time, but was that stick not your father's? I've been most careful not to lose it and have regularly polished the wood to preserve it."

"Father had a few sticks," I lied with a smile. "Ernest, I felt that it was the right time for you to let it go." I didn't add that I was worried he may kiss me!

"You're right. It's been nearly six years and the night terrors are few. Life has been most enjoyable these past few weeks, even if it has been peppered with unfortunate circumstances."

"Let's inspect the bridge up close," I said. "When we are able to leave, will you still accompany us to Denham Hall?" I asked.

"Of course, Ellen. I do have some business to

attend to at the start of next week, but will be able to visit before I head off to Bristol."

"What business have you in Bristol?" I asked.

"I have an investment which has done exceptionally well," he said.

"That's good to hear, considering you've not been making a lot from your security business."

Hamilton laughed. "Indeed, I am most fortunate."

As we reached the bridge, we heard the men working and hammering in nails.

"It's nearly fixed," I said.

"That's a relief." Hamilton approached the men and chatted to them as I observed. He returned. "It will be ready by tomorrow noon," he said. "They need to reinforce it, to ensure it is strong enough for the motorcars and horses and carts.

"Excellent news." I felt a rush of relief as we turned around and made our way back to the house. This time I noticed a gate to our left.

"That's Shaw's cottage," Hamilton said.

"Shall we take a look?" I asked.

He raised his eyebrows. "Are we snooping?"

I laughed. "I simply wish to take a look at the outside, I've no intention of breaking in." I walked up to the door of the dark cottage.

"It was used by their old gardener," Hamilton said.

"Freddie told me it used to be quite pretty but Shaw has not kept up with the gardening."

"I can see that," I said, noticing how overgrown it was. Vines covered many of the windows so I assumed it must be quite dark inside, yet I was dying to go in. I lifted my hand and was about to twist the handle.

"Ellen, it's locked. I locked it myself, having checked the house over to see if The Magpie was hiding inside."

"Of course," I said with a laugh, dropping my hand to my side. I turned to face him. "Anything interesting in there?"

"I was looking for The Magpie. If you wish to stay and investigate on behalf of Mr Doyle, I will let you in. In fact, the key is underneath this pot." He bent down and lifted a terracotta pot to reveal a key. "There's not much inside worth stealing."

I hesitated. My inquisitive nature was pumping. I took a deep breath. "No, I need to step away. All I want to do is to return to Denham Hall." I smiled at him. "You will love it."

"Shall I clean your car and ensure that any water that may have leaked in has been mopped up so we can have a pleasant journey tomorrow?"

"That's an excellent idea," I said and, without thinking, linked my arm into his as we headed back up to Moor House.

I left Hamilton with the motorcar and returned to the house with a smile upon my face. I entered through the kitchen door to find Ivy at the table, preparing the vegetables for the soup.

"It's leek and potato," she said.

I already knew as Joseph had told me.

"And this evening it will be omelette and salad. Conrad suggested slaughtering one of the chickens." She shook her head. "Joseph would never allow that. Those chickens are all named, they've got personalities. Our meat is always bought in, even when he had an old sow back there."

"I've been to the bridge. It's nearly fixed and will be ready for cars by midday tomorrow."

"Thank goodness for that," she said, giving me a grin so wide that I sensed Ivy was eager for me to leave.

"I also saw the house you were telling me about. The one that Shaw lives in. It's a charming little cottage."

"It's a little overgrown. But now I'm older and Joseph is a man, it would be much better for me to live there. Rather than living here in the main house. Part of me regrets not taking it. And it would be easier for me to receive my own guests."

"Does Mr Shaw receive guests?" I asked, making conversation.

She pursed her lips. "I've only seen one person ever go there, other than him." She shook her head. "But I won't say who that was."

I felt a trickle of curiosity and tried to bite my tongue but could not help myself. "Why would their identity need to be kept quiet?"

She looked around her. "Someone had a thing with him, years back."

"Really?" I got the distinct impression that she was referring to a romantic liaison. Maybe it was the woman that Shaw spoke of. That he had once loved.

"If Conrad knew, he'd sack Sid on the spot," Ivy said with a sniff.

I wondered whether the Doyles' marriage had been under strain? After all, it would appear they married after a very short liaison, and only because Winnie was with child, not necessarily because they loved each other.

Thinking of Mr Shaw, I realised it was time for me to check his dressing. I had not seen him since the previous evening. "I will check on my patient to see how he is. Hopefully the doctor will be able to get through tomorrow."

"Sid's lucky you were here, my lady," Ivy said with another wide smile.

I left the room in search of Lottie, who was no

longer in the garden, so I could impart the good news that we could leave the following day. I knew she was desperate to get back to Denham, to discover whether there had been word from Sebastian.

Chapter Fifteen

Whilst attending to Mr Shaw, I had missed luncheon with the family, which I was not at all disappointed about. I sat at a bench before a table, set on the patio, breathing in the fresh air as I ate the soup which Ivy had saved for me with freshly made bread. Lottie sat beside me and Prince bounded around the garden. My dog appeared to have an extensive energy store.

"It's so beautiful and peaceful here," I said, listening to the birds singing in the trees and feeling a mild breeze against my skin.

"I feel much happier knowing we can leave tomorrow," Lottie said.

"I have to agree that could be the reason for my better spirits. And as inquisitive as I am, I'm more than happy to leave this case to the police."

"How was Mr Shaw?" Lottie asked.

"We were discussing The Magpie. He thinks it was likely to be him. He said he's stolen from a few people in Dulverton. Including the grocery store owner's wife, Delia Monroe."

"What did he steal from her?"

"A pearl necklace bearing her initials on the clasp. It was an anniversary present from her husband to celebrate their ten year wedding anniversary and she had bragged about it."

"Not a good idea with a thief in town," Lottie said.

"Jewellery is so personal, unlike money." I placed my spoon in the empty bowl. "Hopefully we can forget all about it tomorrow and return to Phoebe and the girls."

Lottie stood up. "I'll pack most of our things. I want to write Sebastian a letter. I'll ask Mr Doyle for some paper."

I watched Lottie go, wishing with all my heart that she would be reunited with Sebastian, yet also realising how unlikely it was.

I spent the afternoon in much brighter spirits. I took Prince for a walk then sat on a chair under a tree, reading a book taken from Conrad's bookshelf. I relaxed and felt a little guilty that I'd done nothing to further the case, but I knew in my heart I had no desire to pursue the matter.

It was soon time for our evening meal and, having changed and settled Prince in the scullery, I made my way to the dining room with Lottie.

"Ah, welcome, ladies. What have you deduced today?" Purnell asked us.

"Nothing I wish to discuss with you, Lord Purnell," I said.

"Lady Ellen updated me earlier on her thoughts," Conrad said. "I see no need to share them at the dining table."

Ivy delivered our filled plates, placing them in front of us one by one.

"I agree, Father," Robert said. "Let us enjoy the evening. The future may be challenging but let us relax."

"I hear the bridge will be passable tomorrow," Purnell said.

Conrad looked slightly worried. I knew he wanted Purnell to stay in case the amulet was found. He took a deep breath then reached for his wine.

As we ate, I deduced that Ivy was a very good cook. The omelette was light and filled with cheese and mushrooms, accompanied by a varied and colourful salad with scrubbed boiled potatoes covered with a herb infused butter. Whilst I had enjoyed the hotel food I had been given over the weeks and the delights provided by Phoebe's cook at Denham Hall, simple food was a light relief from the rich sauces and fancy dishes I'd eaten over the past couple of months.

"Shall we play cards?" Freddie asked after the dessert of poached pear and cream.

"Lady Ellen may find poker vulgar," Conrad said.

"Not in the slightest," I said. "I played many games with the men at my convalescent home and found poker most thrilling."

"We have chips we can play with," Robert said. "And Father, please can we invite Grace, Joseph and Ivy to join us?"

Conrad hesitated then nodded. "Very well, it will make a more interesting game."

Lottie sat wide-eyed. "Do I have to play?" She appeared rather nervous.

"Not at all," I said.

"I'd quite like to write more, if you have an additional sheet of paper, Mr Doyle?"

"Take as much as you like, lass," he replied.

Lottie left the room as Ivy and Grace came in to clear the table for the game. We were soon all seated and Robert dealt the chips and cards, acting as croupier. Joseph was not present, having declined the invitation.

My heart pounded as we played. The pile of chips before me was becoming greater with every hand. When I said I had played many games, I indeed had and my experience had spanned six years. I had learned to read people and wondered if that skill had assisted me in recent weeks when unravelling mysteries. Every time I took a win from Purnell, I found myself becoming more excited. *Is he reeling me in?* I wondered, realising I needed to remain calm.

Conrad and Grace were already out of the game and Ivy had left to sit with Shaw. Freddie pushed all of her chips forward once the river had been laid. Smoke rose from her cigar as she gazed into Purnell's eyes. With the smoke from Conrad's cigarettes, the aroma of wine and the music coming from the gramophone, the Doyle dining room had the feel of a jazz club.

I checked my hand, doubting that three tens would win the pile of chips before me, so folded. Purnell was nonchalant. I read that as him hiding the fact that he had a winning hand.

Hamilton placed his cards on the table. "A flush." He grinned at Purnell.

"I'm out," Freddie said, discarding her cards.

I could tell by Purnell's eyes that he had him. "Royal flush."

Hamilton nodded and sat back. "You got me."

"It's me and you, Lady Ellen," Purnell said with a smile. "Unless you wish to retire?"

"If it was real money, I would have bowed out a few hands back," I said.

"You won't want to lose face?" he said.

I felt my teeth clench together. "Deal," I said.

Robert laughed as he dealt the cards. "I've not had this much fun for months."

"I'm enjoying observing this tension," Freddie said suggestively, looking at me then to Purnell, before leaning into Hamilton.

I ignored her comment as Robert continued to place the cards.

I picked my cards up. *Two aces,* I thought.

"All in," Purnell said, pushing his chips into the centre of the table. "Let's make it interesting. Winner takes all."

I thought I had him, assuming he probably had nothing. He was a reckless man. The overwhelming need to beat him took over as I pushed all of my chips into the centre of the table. My heart pounded as the cards were turned over, but there were more aces.

Purnell grinned at me. "Show me what you have," he said once all the cards were on the table.

I placed the two aces in front of me.

He nodded with a smile. "Same."

"It's a draw," Grace said clapping.

"It has to be determined by the kicker," Purnell said.

I smiled as I placed a queen on the table.

He placed the King. "Got you."

Freddie laughed loudly, puffing a plume of cigar smoke above us.

I caught Hamilton's eye and he smiled at me and I felt myself calm a little. It was only a silly game of cards, but the look in Purnell's eyes at having beaten me riled me up. I took in a deep breath. Why was this man constantly trying to get under my skin?

I stood up. "Thank you for the entertaining evening, it was most enjoyable." I smiled, after all it was only a game. "I will retire. It's been nice to spend time with you all," I said and left the room.

After collecting Prince from the scullery, I decided to take him for a walk. I wanted a period of solitude before bed. I was looking forward to taking him back to Ashcombe Hall where he could run off the leash and enjoy the freedom he was used to.

In the garden, Prince tugged at his leash and I decided to go off the grounds. I walked down the lane to see how much they had progressed with the bridge. The light was dimming so I knew I only had about half an hour before darkness fell. I reached Shaw's cottage. I thought I heard something behind me and turned, spotting a rabbit move out from the bushes. I smiled as it hopped away, with a flash of white from its rear. I turned back to the cottage and, having seen no one, I opened the gate, which squeaked, then walked up the garden path.

I reached the terracotta pot and my inquisitiveness took over as I bent down to move it, retrieving the key hidden beneath. My hand shook as I opened the door. Once inside the small entrance, I did not lock the door in case I needed to make a speedy exit.

I turned to Prince. "Stay here," I whispered to him at he sat on the mat. "Your feet are muddy." The light was dimming but I could not light a candle in the cottage, which appeared not to have electricity, as I did not want to draw any attention to the fact that I was there.

I found the kitchen and went inside. It was clean, maybe someone had been in and tidied it for him. It was so neat. I entered the lounge area. It was also extremely neat, if a little sparse. I found a bureau. I stared at it, hesitating, then stepped forward. After turning the key which was in the lock, I lifted the lid. I took a deep breath. Everything inside was orderly. Remembering that when I had spoken to Shaw, he had talked of once being in love with a woman, I wondered whether he had kept some sort of memorabilia. I did not know how relevant it would be to the missing amulet and shook my head. I guessed I was simply being incredibly nosey. I was about to close the lid when I spotted a pile of letters, tied in string.

"Don't," I whispered to myself as I picked them up, my hands shaking. But I could not resist, justifying it by telling myself I was investigating the matter. I opened the letter with a trembling hand, and read:

Sid,

I love you. You know I want us to be together.

I jumped as Prince barked from the porch.

I turned front, hearing the door open and then close. I quickly flipped the paper over to see who it was from. As soon as I had seen the sender write *All my love, W xx.* I stuffed the letter back and closed the lid.

Just as I thought. Shaw and Winnie.

"Are we being nosey?"

I swung around to find myself facing Lord Purnell. I'd recognised his voice but could not see his features, merely his outline.

"I..."

"You are, aren't you?" he said. The room appeared extra dark as he stood before the window, blocking out what little light there was. It made him appear as a menacing shadow. I gulped. I did not want him to know I was intimidated.

"Did you follow me?" I demanded.

"Following someone is a lesser crime than breaking into private property. Are you The Magpie?"

"Highly amusing, Lord Purnell, and I did not break in, I used the key!" I lifted it.

He moved towards me. "Why?" he asked.

"I was worried about the cat," I said, remembering Ivy mentioning that Shaw had a black cat named Fly.

"What cat?" He took another step towards me and was now close enough that I could smell the faint aroma of his musky cologne, somewhat subtler than Conrad's.

"Shaw's cat has not been fed." I gestured to the door. "That's why I left Prince in the porch." I breathed out, feeling I had a plausible excuse for being there. "I thought the cat may have been locked in."

"How caring of you." He looked over my shoulder. "Find anything interesting in the bureau?"

I remained silent, realising he had spotted me. It was fruitless to deny it.

He took one step closer and I could smell the faint waft of sherry on his breath.

I took a step backwards so the bureau was against my lower back. "I think we should leave." I gestured for him to go.

He leaned forwards so that I could see his face, the stubble of the day and the whites of his eyes. He stared at me and I became acutely aware that we were alone. And that I could be face to face with the man who had stabbed Shaw.

"For my dignity?" I added in a steady voice as Prince barked from the porch.

Purnell took two steps backwards and chuckled.

"Of course, my lady." He gave a comical bow. "It would not do for us to spotted alone. What a scandal!" He turned for the door and I let out a long breath, steadying myself against the bureau.

I left, locking the front door but did not deposit the key underneath the pot. I planned to hand it to Hamilton for safekeeping. Although I would have to confess to being incredibly nosey myself. Especially when I intended to leave first thing the following day. As I walked down the path with Prince, Purnell was waiting for me at the gate.

Prince barked, pulling at his leash as a black cat sped out of the bushes.

I gave a small curt smile to Purnell. "Ah, Mr Shaw's cat!"

He chuckled. "I'm taking an evening stroll across the bridge, would you care to join me?"

"No, thank you," I said and briskly walked away in the direction of the main house. As the light faded and the house came into view bats fluttered above and I shuddered.

Chapter Sixteen

"Goodnight, Ellen," Lottie said with a yawn from the bed next to me. I had updated her on the letter I'd found confirming my suspicion that Shaw had been having an affair with Mrs Doyle. As I attempted to sleep, it nagged at me. I felt it was incredibly relevant but could not see why it would result in him being stabbed, because surely Conrad Doyle would have sacked Shaw, as Ivy had said, if he knew. And there was no point in Conrad stealing his own belongings, quite apart from the fact that he had an alibi. Lottie had heard him speaking to Robert just before the attack. Was the amulet a fake? And that was the secret Robert and Conrad were discussing before the attack? I felt a dull ache in the pit of my stomach. What if, as Winnie's daughter had suggested, her death had not been a tragic accident?

What if Shaw was suspicious of the way Winnie had died and the theft was a cover for someone trying to silence him? I tossed and turned as my mind threw up different scenarios. Was Sid Shaw in danger? Should I alert Hamilton and ask him to protect him? My mind raced and I attempted to calm myself. Was there not a thief but a failed murderer in the house?

"The bridge will be cleared in the morning," I whispered to myself. I wanted to distance myself, to leave and forget all about this place and its inhabitants.

Prince slept at the end of the bed and, with the rhythm of his snores, I felt my heartbeat slow and I finally drifted off to sleep.

I was woken at just after four o'clock by a wail. My body froze as the sound seemed to pierce the still of the night. It sent a painful shiver down my back and was a cry I had heard before, many years before. The sound of a man dogged by nightmares, by those atrocities he had witnessed in the war – it was Hamilton. As I lay there, I stared at the ceiling, not knowing what to do. Would it be appropriate for me to go to his room in a private house? This was no hospital or convalescent home. I sat up, leaning on my elbows.

"What's that?" Lottie asked with a fearful voice. "A ghost?"

I turned to her and pulled the covers off my body, swinging my legs so I was sitting on the edge of the bed facing her. "It's Ernest having a nightmare," I said. "Nothing to worry about. I will see if I can rouse him by knocking on his door." I stood up and glanced in the mirror of the dressing table. I could not go in what I was wearing. I hurried to put my dress on then fumbled in the dark for my shoes, by which time the wailing had ceased.

I opened the bedroom door, looking along the landing to where Hamilton's room was. I stepped out, then hesitated, wondering whether I should continue to Hamilton's room or return to my bed. I jumped as I heard someone whisper in my ear, so close the breath brushed my lobe.

"Ellen."

I swung around with my hand to my chest as my heart beat hard. It was Purnell. He smiled down at me, wearing a vest which showed off the strong physique of his torso.

"I was just..." I stammered, realising that if I said I was headed to Hamilton's room it would look most inappropriate. I wished I'd remained in our room as I assumed Hamilton had returned to sleep.

"Freddie Doyle has made many a man cry out at night," Purnell said, gesturing towards Hamilton's room.

I felt incensed at Purnell's ridiculous insinuation, but a trickle of doubt seeped into my mind. There was scratching at my bedroom door as Prince's claws prised it open.

"If you will excuse me, Lord Purnell. I need to take my dog outside." I placed my hand on Prince's collar. "And before you ask, no I do not require your company."

I was enraged as I headed for the staircase with Prince at heel. I heard a door close along the landing and assumed Purnell had returned to his room. I slowed, feeling my heartbeat follow suit. I took the stairs, my hand running along the smooth dark banister. The front door was unbolted. I guessed Conrad felt the need for high security had passed, considering he had lost his priceless amulet.

Once outside, I felt calmer and breathed in the cool air. The sky was clear and it was a full moon with the garden bathed in soft light. Wildlife rustled in the bushes and a vixen cried out in the distance. I felt the chill of the air, having left without a coat. I chastened myself for allowing the incorrigible Lord Purnell to play with my feelings. But still, I was also shocked at the jealousy I had felt, imagining Hamilton with Freddie. Even though I knew an upstanding man such as he would do no such thing. I carried along the drive in the still of the night, then stopped. In the distance was Hamilton crossing the gardens. I sped up, feeling the wet dew on the grass hit my bare legs, for I'd not had time to put on stockings. I did not want to call out to him. He turned around, probably hearing myself and Prince crossing the lawn. He stopped and then, as he strode towards us, I slowed my step – although Prince of course continued to bound up to him.

"Ellen, what are you doing out here?" he asked me as Prince ran around him in circles.

"I was about to ask the same." I paused. "I heard you cry out."

He ran a hand through his hair, unruly from sleep. "It was only to be expected."

"It was a night terror?"

"Yes. I was watching my poor men, being blasted into the air. Unable to help. I decided to come out here, in the quiet of the night, to remind myself the world is at peace."

"I'm sorry, I feel responsible for tossing away your stick."

"It's for the best, Ellen. I'm much stronger. It was the right time."

I felt myself warm in the chilly air, realising how silly I had been to allow Purnell to upset me. I then froze for a moment as we heard a voice.

We both turned towards the sound.

"That will be Joseph in his shed," Hamilton said. "He's a man of few words but talks to himself often in there."

"In the middle of the night?" I asked.

"He arises at four most mornings. I think he prefers the quiet. As soon as the sun rises he sees to his chickens, otherwise the cockerel makes an awful noise and wakes the house."

I walked towards the shed and Hamilton followed. Normally he would suggest I should not be so nosey, but I guessed at the back of his mind, as was with mine, there was a mystery to solve.

As we neared the shed, we heard Joseph speaking in a clear purposeful tone.

"Father, do you even see me?" he said.

A chill filled my bones. "Is he conversing with the dead?" I whispered to Hamilton as I stroked Prince's back, hoping he would not bark.

"No, but Joseph may believe he is," Hamilton whispered back.

"It must have been so sad for him growing up without a father. My mama died when I was young. It's terribly difficult for a child."

I inched around the outside of the shed until I saw Joseph, who had his back to the window. The interior was lit by a candle and he was whittling out a piece of wood with a small sharp knife. On the bench was a finished piece in the shape of an otter.

I looked up at Hamilton. "You don't think he stabbed Shaw?"

"I really don't know," he said as we stepped back. "Do you want to get involved with this family and its secrets? We will be leaving later today."

"You're right," I said. "I need to focus on our trip to Denham." I kept the discovery of the letter I had seen in Shaw's cottage the previous evening to myself. I also made no mention of the key which I still had concealed in my dress pocket, deciding to quietly return it when I took Prince for a walk before our journey. "I think we should get some more sleep," I said. "We need to be alert for the drive."

We moved away and crossed the lawn. My dog whined at me.

"I'll clean Prince's paws in the scullery and feed him before returning to our room," I said.

When we reached the house, Hamilton locked the front door and took the stairs to his room, whilst I headed along the passageway towards the scullery with Prince trotting after me.

Inside, the room appeared sinister in the dim light with rabbits and pheasants hanging from meat hooks from the ceiling. The cast iron stove looked eerie inside the shadowy inglenook. I quickly cleaned my dog's mucky feet then stopped as I heard footsteps. *Is that Hamilton?* I then groaned to myself. *I hope it's not Purnell.* My heartbeat quickened and I stood back into the shadows to discover that it was in fact Joseph who passed. However, he did not enter the scullery, but continued along the tiled passageway with something tucked underneath his arm. I moved forward to follow then hesitated. *Don't get involved,* I told myself and filled Prince's bowl with some of his Spratt's Dog Cakes and placed it before him.

As he chomped away, I looked to where I had seen Joseph. In the distance, I heard his footsteps on the staircase. It was too much for me to resist. "You stay here, boy," I whispered. "I'll be back in a short while." I removed my shoes, padded into the passageway and followed the sound of Joseph's footsteps. I reached the upper floor and heard movement above, on the stairs to the attic. I quickly yet silently took the stairs in my bare feet and glanced around the corner to see an open door, with candlelight flickering inside. I peered between a gap in the door. This was not the attic room where Shaw was stabbed. Joseph was inside the room which I presumed contained Conrad's artwork, the door that had supposedly been locked since the day Conrad moved in with the Firth family. *Surely no one's supposed to go inside?* I thought. Realising I would be unable to follow him in there, I padded back down the stairs. Behind me, I heard the click of the attic door closing, so I sped up until I was on the ground floor and back inside the scullery.

Hiding behind the door, I held my breath, listening

to my own heart thudding as I waited for Joseph to pass. Prince had found his bone and was chewing on it when the man passed. I peered around the door. Joseph headed out of the tradesman's entrance and before he closed the door, I heard the cockerel cry.

"What are you doing?"

I jumped and turned, putting my hand to my heart. I breathed out slowly as I looked into Lottie's eyes. With the long nightdress, she appeared rather like a ghost.

"You scared me," I said.

"What's going on?" she hissed. "I was worried. I've been waiting on the landing for you and saw Ernest go to his room but you weren't with him."

"I've been upstairs. Joseph went into the locked room," I whispered to her.

"What locked room?"

"The one in the attic, opposite the one Shaw was stabbed inside. I want to go in and have a look."

Her eyes widened. "You mean, right now?"

"Yes, but I don't have a key."

Lottie visibly relaxed. "Maybe ask Conrad Doyle for one in the morning. Come upstairs now, I need my sleep."

"No, I need to go to the room immediately. And I know someone who has a key to every door of this house. Follow me."

Lottie sighed from behind me. I knew she found the house spooky and wanted us both to be locked inside our bedroom until the sun was fully up. I left Prince snoring below the scullery table, with his bone underneath one paw.

Upstairs, I knocked gently on Hamilton's bedroom door.

"Who is it?" he said from inside, sounding rather worried.

"It's me, Ellen."

The door swung open with much speed.

"And me," Lottie said, letting out a giggle.

"I need access to the attic room next to the one Shaw was found in," I whispered, "containing Conrad's artwork."

"I'll be right out." Hamilton did not question me but shut the door, presumably whilst he fetched the keys for he was still dressed from his pre-dawn walk.

"You don't have to come," I said to Lottie.

"I don't like being on my own in this house," she said. "But I'll change, I nearly tripped in this nightgown."

Hamilton was soon beside me with the set of keys and when we reached our room, Lottie was opening the door having slipped her dress on. As we walked along the landing, I explained to Hamilton what I had witnessed as the sun emitted its first glow over the top of the trees, filling the grounds with an orange hue. Lottie and Hamilton followed me up to the attic.

When we reached the door to the art room, I stepped aside as Hamilton pulled the bundle of keys from his pocket. I waited in anticipation until he found the correct one which turned in the lock.

We entered and I stopped, for it was too dark to see anything. I fumbled my way across to the window whilst Hamilton locked the door behind us. I pulled back the thick curtain to allow the growing sunlight to enter the room. I guessed the drapes were thick to prevent the rays from damaging the paintings. When I turned around, I found the room was not at all dusty. Far from being out of bounds, someone had clearly been in there often, admiring the art. And I guessed that someone was Joseph Wood.

I approached the first painting, which was signed by Conrad Doyle. I suddenly felt sorry for the fellow. The artwork was more than good – it was beautiful. For the man to consider he had lost his gift was a travesty. There were a few landscapes displaying the beauty of South West England. But most were portraits, capturing with skill the emotions of his subjects. I carried on around the room. One portrait was of a woman who shared a likeness with Freddie, and I guessed it was Mrs Winnie Doyle, Conrad's late wife. If Shaw had been in love with her, I could understand why. At the back of the room was another painting, covered by a cloth. I approached it and removed the cover and gasped. It was of a very beautiful and young woman, laid on a chaise longue with a strategically placed sheet, which did not completely cover her womanly attributes. It was as if she smiled at us, her eyes alight with blonde tresses cascading over bare shoulders.

"Is that...?" Lottie trailed off.

"I do believe it is," Hamilton said, blushing before lowering his gaze.

Conrad had captured a look of longing, of love, of devotion in her eyes. I took a deep breath as I was drawn to her smile, a bright smile with a large gap between her front teeth.

Chapter Seventeen

"Well, that Ivy Wood is a dark horse, getting her clothes off like that," Lottie said as she stared at the picture.

"And she told me he hadn't painted since he arrived here!" I said.

"Indeed," Hamilton said thoughtfully. "An unreliable witness." He scanned the room. "It looks as though he worked with wood, too."

In one corner was a cabinet housing a selection of carvings.

"They're really good," I said. "But I do not feel they are Conrad's work, but Joseph's."

"Look at all them cupboards," Lottie said. "I wonder what's inside."

"Let's check," I said.

Lottie and I tried the cupboards. Most of them held sketchbooks, dried up paint pots and brushes. All but one opened.

"Have you a key for this cupboard?" I asked Hamilton. "They all have their own key, except this one."

He gestured towards the locked cupboard door. "I have no keys that small."

"Let us fetch Prince," I said, "and go to our room to discuss the matter before the rest of the house wakes."

We left the room as we found it and headed downstairs to hear a voice floating from the scullery.

Ivy looked up at us as we entered the room, whilst petting Prince. "Such a lovely dog. I wish I had one."

"Prince is a faithful companion," I said, staring at the woman who I had just seen languishing half-dressed on a chaise lounge, albeit in oil on canvas. I noticed Hamilton blush, and guessed he was also picturing Ivy undressed. It was an image difficult to eradicate from one's mind. It was possible that Ivy was merely modelling for Conrad but as I looked into her eyes, remembering how they were depicted in the portrait, I deduced that she'd had an affair with him, under the same roof he shared with his wife. But on the other hand, his wife had possibly been in the arms of his butler, Shaw. A much younger man. Did Winnie Doyle ever see the painting of Ivy Wood? Is that why she sought solace with Shaw? Why did Conrad still have the painting? It was understandable that Joseph had covered it over. How did he feel about it? And more importantly, what was locked in the cupboard? I had so many questions which I ached to have answers to.

Ivy stood up. "You're all up early."

"I rose after a bad dream," Hamilton said.

"We're keen to be on our way as soon as the bridge is fixed," I said.

"I need to collect Prince," Lottie added. "Come along, boy."

Back in the bedroom, Lottie and Hamilton followed me in.

"What time are we leaving?" Lottie asked.

"We need to discover what lies in that cupboard," I said. "Then we'll be on our way, assuming the bridge is safe to cross."

"Do you want me to ask Conrad for the key?" Hamilton asked.

I looked at the clock on the mantelpiece. "It's still before six. We will have to wait until seven at least. It's an ideal place to hide something, a room no-one is allowed in."

"Conrad seemed pretty sure no one goes in there," Hamilton said. "Otherwise, I'm sure he would have asked me to check it when I searched the house for The Magpie. He specifically said there was no reason to check that room as he had the only key, which is on this set." He lifted the bunch of keys.

"Joseph clearly cut another," I said.

"Ivy was so beautiful," Lottie said. "She looked so young."

"She was only twenty-one when she came to Moor House," I said.

"Do you think she and Conrad were in love?" Lottie asked.

"Possibly," I said.

"It may have been innocent," Hamilton added. "He is an artist, he could add details which may not have been there in reality."

"I hope we get to the bottom of this," I said.

"Are you thinking of staying?" Lottie asked in a meek voice. I knew she was looking forward to leaving, as was I.

I hesitated and looked at Hamilton and then back to Lottie.

"Phoebe will be worried about us," Lottie continued. "She must be wondering where we've got to."

"I know, but what if the amulet is hidden in that cupboard?" I gestured to Hamilton. "Ernest will not be paid unless it's found."

"Please don't worry about me," Hamilton said. "I'm not sure I wish to accept payment under the circumstances."

I smiled at Lottie. "Let's open the cupboard and if my hunch is correct, the amulet will be in there and we can leave!"

"Are you able to pick a lock?" I asked Hamilton.

"It's not ethical for us to break into that cupboard," he said.

"You're right," I said. "Come along let's wash and dress in fresh clothes and seek Conrad out. The sooner the better."

Half an hour later, we found that Conrad had risen early and was in his study, drinking tea and eating fresh bread.

"Mr Doyle, we've made progress on the case," I said as we entered.

Conrad's face brightened as he leaned back in his chair. "Yes?"

"I believe the amulet may be hidden in your art room," I said as Hamilton and Lottie followed me in.

He frowned and sat up straight. "No one's been in there for years. Are you sure?"

I nodded. "There's a locked cupboard inside."

"And how do you know this?" he asked.

"As part of my investigation, I accessed the room."

"You went into the art room?" He seemed somewhat unhappy as he stood up from the desk.

"May I say, Mr Doyle, you are a most skilled artist," I said hoping to calm him.

"I think they're amazing," Lottie added.

"You were in there too?" he said with a frown.

"Your paintings are wasted locked away," Hamilton said.

Conrad's face turned red. "You've all been in there?"

I lowered my voice. "I followed Joseph up there. He let himself in."

Conrad sat back in his seat. "I thought there was only one key, and that is the one you hold, Hamilton. What is this cupboard you speak of?"

"There are many in the room, but one is locked," Hamilton said.

"I've no key to any such cupboard." Conrad reached into his drawer and pulled out a pocket knife. "But this should do the trick. If you really believe the amulet is in there, let's find out."

We followed Conrad out of the study, along the corridor, past the kitchen and the scullery on our way to the servants' stairs.

Conrad took a deep breath when we reached the room. He gestured at Hamilton. "Open the door, man."

Hamilton went in before us and pulled the drapes to allow the now brilliant sunshine to illuminate the room.

I placed my hand on Conrad's arm. "Has it been some time since you've been in here?"

"Not since I moved in. Twenty-four years ago," he replied, although I considered that to be a lie, considering the painting we had viewed of Ivy Wood.

He stood wide-eyed. "It appears Joseph has been taking care of them," he said in a choked whisper. "I left them covered and piled against the walls." He wandered around the room, with his hand to his mouth, looking aghast at his pieces.

"I'm sure you can see these now from an objective point of view, considering the passage of time. They're beautiful," I said.

Conrad took a deep breath as if composing himself. He frowned and pointed to the carvings in the cabinet in the corner. "I don't recognise those."

"We believe they're Joseph's," Hamilton said, hammering home that the young man had been using the room.

Conrad nodded. "Of course."

"He said to us that you were an amazing artist. I assumed he'd merely heard that." I looked around at the paintings. "Clearly he said it from the experience of looking at your work."

"Show me the cupboard in question," Conrad said gruffly, clearly not wishing to discuss his gift any further.

Lottie tapped on it. "This one."

He released his knife from the casing, dug into the lock and forced it open. It creaked. We all looked on in anticipation.

Conrad peered inside and remained still.

"Is it there?" Lottie asked.

He slowly shook his head. "No. But it was. There's something else in there, though." He stepped back. "It's a whittling knife."

"The kind used to carve wood?" Hamilton asked gesturing at Joseph's work.

I approached the cupboard and looked inside. At the back of the white painted cupboard was a blood-crusted knife and at the front a reddish stain in an oval shape. I stepped back so Hamilton and Lottie could also observe what we had uncovered.

"The blood stain is in the shape of the amulet," Hamilton said.

Conrad groaned. "It was here! I wish you had forced the lock when you found it. Did anyone see you come up here?"

"Joseph must have seen you outside the room," Hamilton said to me. "No one touch the knife. It may have his fingerprints on it and will prove he stabbed Shaw."

"With the bridge now fixed, he may be making his

escape," I added. "What's this?" An envelope was propped inside and I gently pulled it out.

"Open it," Conrad said.

I did as he requested.

"It's a ticket," Lottie said, looking over my shoulder.

"Joseph is indeed planning to escape," I said holding it up. "It's a ticket to India."

"What shall we do with it?" Lottie asked.

"Take it. We don't want him leaving the country," Hamilton said.

Conrad ran a hand through his hair. "Why the blazes didn't I order a search of the entire house myself?" He swung around. "With it having been hidden in this cupboard, it proves that someone in this house is the thief and not The Magpie. Get everyone together in the lounge. I'm going to find who it is and demand the thing back."

"Take a breath, Conrad," Hamilton said. "It was clearly Joseph."

"Ellen saw him come into this room," Lottie added. "It's his knife covered in blood."

"It's not him!" Conrad said shaking his head. "Someone is framing him by using his knife."

I wanted to go through the suspects with Conrad in a calm manner before he needlessly accused his family and staff. I was unsure as to why he would not accept Joseph as a suspect, even though the evidence pointed at him and Joseph had no verifiable alibi.

"Let us have tea and discuss the facts logically," I said in a gentle voice.

"Check everyone's still here," Conrad said gruffly to Hamilton.

"Of course," Hamilton said, not baulking at Conrad's order. After all, the case was now in its final stages.

"Invite everyone to meet us in the drawing room in half an hour," Conrad asked him. "Let's go to my Study," he said to Lottie and myself.

Chapter Eighteen

Lottie and I sat in Conrad's study. We had collected Prince from our room and Lottie was at the end of the desk, stroking his head, whilst I sat directly opposite Conrad. He remained silent for a while, as if in contemplation and all we could hear was the tick of the clock sitting upon the mantelpiece of the small fireplace.

Conrad sat forward, his hands pressed together. "So tell me, who do you think has the amulet?"

"Joseph," Lottie said slowly.

"It's not possible." Conrad sat back in his chair.

"He's been using the room where the amulet and murder weapon were hidden," I said. "And you saw his carvings with your own eyes. And it was a whittling knife which was covered, we assume, in your butler's blood!"

"No. It can't be," Conrad said.

"But I saw Joseph enter the room at dawn."

"Someone's framing him. You've been here for a couple of days and discovered he uses that room. Anyone else could have found that out. Go through the other suspects."

I glanced at Lottie and she shrugged.

"If you wish," I said, missing our usual use of a notebook. "I'll start with your family. Robert, as you know, has an alibi."

Conrad frowned.

I gestured to Lottie. "You were overheard discussing a secret with him at the time of the theft."

Lottie blushed and I nodded at her.

"I was passing your study, Mr Doyle, and heard raised voices," she said. "I heard him say 'Father, we have to tell the others' and you said 'no, never.'" She lowered her head as if she had been eavesdropping.

Conrad took a sharp breath. "Indeed, yes."

"Do you think this secret you share with Robert could have a bearing on the case?" I asked.

"No, absolutely not. What else do you have?"

"Apart from that, I don't see what motive Robert would have other than if he wishes to leave Dulverton with his sweetheart, Grace, of whom you do not approve."

"My son is not courting that woman." He glared

at me.

"It has not escaped anyone's attention that he is very much in love with her and he could want to run away with the young woman, as you clearly do not approve."

"She is merely his latest fancy. He'll soon realise she's not of the right class for him."

I glanced at Lottie who pursed her lips, and realised she was likening his attitude to that of Sebastian's parents.

"What else do you have?" he asked me with a frown.

"Freddie," I said.

"My daughter?" He shook his head. "She's no interest in such things."

From what I had gleaned about Freddie, Conrad was probably right, but then would she relish hurting her father? Making him suffer? I had seen no evidence of a strong father-daughter bond.

"She may wish to return the piece to Egypt, where it originated," I suggested.

Conrad laughed. "She complains about the journey to here from London. I can't see her taking a boat and train for such a long trip."

"And we have Ivy," I said looking at him intently. "There have been hints that she has an affection for you."

"What makes you say that?" he demanded.

I took my chance to be direct with the fellow. "You told us you had not painted since you came to Moor House. Yet you must have because there's a portrait of her in the attic."

"Is there?" he asked.

"She's not wearing much," Lottie added.

"Um. Yes." He sat back, blustering. "I painted it some years ago." He wiped his brow.

"We can tell that, she looks a lot younger," Lottie added.

"Why did you paint her?" I asked.

He shook his head. "We sat up one evening. Um ... I'd had too much to drink. Winnie was away. We discussed my art, I said I missed painting." He looked down at his hands. "Ivy said she'd love to have her portrait done."

"I see," I said. I did not have to ask him any further questions. The guilt on his face said it all, and so did the look in Ivy's eyes that he had captured so well with his brush.

He puffed out. "What a mess. It was stupid of me to keep the painting. I didn't think anyone would see it, locked away in that room."

"It's rather large, it must have taken some time to perfect," I said.

"My wife was on an extended trip," he said and looked up. "I trust this will go no further?"

"Of course not." I shot a look to Lottie then turned back to Conrad. "It's a beautiful piece of art, you captured the emotion of the moment," I added trying to sound a little less judgmental.

He sighed. "You think after all these years Ivy would strike back at me for dropping her?"

"From my own observation, I would say Ivy has much respect for you." I said. "But an inner passion can drive a person to extreme actions."

He stood up and looked out of the window. "I provided a home for her and her son! And still do. She's a lot to thank me for."

"Did your wife find out?" I asked.

"Of course not," he said although I got the feeling Conrad was not telling me the complete truth.

"Joseph may have wished to punish you for seducing his mother," I said. "It could have been the motive for stealing the amulet, a way to hurt you. A punishment."

He shook his head. "No. I'm positive, it was not him." He turned around. "What else do you have?"

I felt that Conrad was knocking everyone off my list one by one. It appeared that, whilst he was convinced someone in his household had stolen the amulet, he was loathe to let any of them take the blame.

"Lord Purnell," I said. "He is an obvious candidate."

"No, he's waiting for the amulet to be found so that he can purchase it."

"We'll soon see, if he stays after the bridge is fixed," Lottie said.

"I tell you," Conrad said. "The man is serious about wanting the amulet."

"And Grace?" I said. "She's clearly a disgruntled ex-employee."

Conrad narrowed his eyes. "You know, I think it's her. Getting her own back on me for sending her away from here and me not approving of her seduction of my son!" He checked the time on the clock. "Hopefully everyone is waiting for us in the drawing room. Let's go."

As I watched Conrad leave the room, I considered that I also had him in my mind as a suspect. Creating the illusion of a theft in order to stab the man who had been romancing his wife behind his back. *But does he even know about the affair?* I thought. I certainly had no intention of telling him if he didn't.

In the drawing room, Shaw was sitting in Conrad's armchair with a blanket across his legs. He was looking a lot healthier now, with colour in his face. Everyone else sat on settees and chairs, apart from Conrad who stood by the fireplace. Poor Prince was back in the scullery.

Conrad swung around and then gestured in a large circle. "Someone in this room stole the amulet."

I focused on Joseph for his reaction, but he was also scanning the room and his eyes stopped at Purnell and narrowed. I too looked at the man.

Lord Purnell sat up straight in the wooden chair he was seated on and looked Joseph back in the eyes. "I can assure you, it was not me!"

Conrad sighed. "Sadly, as much as I would want it to be a stranger, the thief is someone who knows this house exceptionally well."

Shaw looked nervously around the room, and I felt sorry for him, considering the man was waiting to face the person who had stabbed him.

Robert frowned. "Surely, Father, you've not included me in your accusation. Your own flesh and blood?"

"And what of me, brother dear?" Freddie said. "I too am flesh and blood."

Robert regarded her. "Sister, you're a much-changed woman. Your clothes are old, your hair has not been cut. I take it you have not a penny to your name for you shun a decent match. And you're barefooted like a beggar on the street! You have the makings of a thief."

"I've absolutely no interest in the amulet or what happened to it. And how dare you judge me by the clothes I wear. So what if I have no wish to follow the crowd. I can assure you, my clothes may not be of the latest fashion, but they are clean and of immense quality." She paused as she eyed me, then turned back to her brother and spoke in a quieter voice. "I do not wear shoes as I want to feel the world beneath my feet. And how dare you refer to me shunning a decent match." She gestured to Grace. "While you are laying down with the vicar's daughter who you feel is beneath you."

"Stop!" Conrad shouted. "Remember our family name."

"Listen to the man speak," Freddie said, gesturing towards him. "It was Mother's family who lived here. Not the Doyles. You do not respect her memory." She shot a look of accusation towards Ivy. "Because of you!"

"Keep me out of your arguments." Ivy shook her head. "What would Mrs Doyle have said if she were here to witness this?"

"As if you cared about my mother," Freddie said and stood up. "You as good as killed her."

"What's that supposed to mean?" Ivy said as her mouth fell open.

Freddie pouted at Ivy. "You're a bitter woman, wanting what you can't have, and it would not surprise me if you pushed our mother down that bank."

"That's enough!" Conrad shouted. "No one leaves this house until the amulet is returned to me. Now get out, all of you. If any of you leave this property, I'll presume your guilt and send the police after you."

"We're under house arrest?" Purnell asked with his hand to his chest in a theatrical fashion.

"Call it what you like," Conrad said.

Lottie whispered to me. "Can we still leave though?"

I did not answer as everyone filed out. Ivy helped Shaw. Shortly there was only Hamilton, Lottie, Conrad and myself in the room.

Conrad shut the drawing room door and then turned to us. "I need you to discover what happened."

"I think you should speak to Joseph," I said, "rather than accusing your own family."

He took a deep breath. "I don't believe it was him. I know I'm pushing everyone away. Please, Lady Ellen, bring this matter to a swift conclusion." He opened the door and left the room.

Lottie looked to me and then to Hamilton and back to me again. "Please, can we go back to Denham Hall? Conrad Doyle isn't worth working for. He owes you money, Ernest. He won't pay you. I want to go." Her chin quivered.

I knew she longed to post her letters to Sebastian and to discover where he was. I felt guilty about that. "We're in the last stages of locating the amulet," I assured her. "I can feel it."

Hamilton nodded. "We need to settle this, the three of us."

Lottie hung her head and sniffed. "If we must."

"But we could do with a break," I said. "You and I will go into Tiverton, to buy some supplies and place a call through to Denham Hall. How about that?" I said.

Lottie nodded silently.

I turned to Hamilton. "I worry about Shaw. Would you mind awfully remaining here and keeping a watchful eye on him?"

"Of course. Whilst we are waiting to discover who stole from Conrad, he is waiting to discover which person in this house, who he has likely known for some time, stabbed him."

"Wouldn't it be good if we discovered it was Lord Purnell?" I said.

"I do not trust the man," Hamilton said.

"I like him," Lottie said in a small voice. "He's funny."

It did not surprise me that Lottie found him entertaining, yet he made me feel extremely uneasy.

Chapter Nineteen

Lottie appeared nervous as we put our hats on and prepared to set off for Tiverton. Prince whined. I felt he was also tiring of Moor House and probably hankered for his life back at Ashcombe Hall, where he had the run of the land and spent his days chasing rabbits. I felt for Lottie, and I also had an attack of nerves: what if Phoebe had not received any letters for her from Sebastian? Or worse, she had received a letter and once opened, the contents would break Lottie's heart.

Downstairs, I took Lottie's hand as we exited via the servants' entrance. "Whatever we discover today, you are a strong and intelligent woman with a bright future ahead of you."

"Thank you, Ellen," she said with a weak smile.

Hamilton appeared behind us and Prince sniffed at

his shoes. "I've spoken to Conrad. I've assured him that you are not visiting the police on your trip." He looked me in the eye. "I'm sorry, Ellen, if that was your intention."

"I have no plans to alert the police until I have hard evidence," I said.

"There's a knife covered in blood," Lottie pointed out.

"Shaw's on the mend. The doctor has been and was pleased everything is healing." Hamilton smiled at me. "Dr Jones asked me to extend his thanks for your excellent nursing skills."

I smiled. "Even though I have not enjoyed our stay here, I am glad I was here to be of help whilst the bridge was blocked."

"And of course," Hamilton added. "With no one at the house wishing to press any charges, there's not an awful lot the police can do!"

As we stood at the entrance, we heard raised voices coming from the direction of the stable.

"Is that Grace?" Lottie asked.

I took her hand and we walked slowly over so we could better hear. Hamilton remained by the door with Prince. As well as Grace, we heard the voice of a man.

"You have brought shame on our family," the man bellowed as we heard the horse neigh.

"Father, there was nothing I could do," Grace said.

"And I'm stuck here. I'm permitted to return the horse and cart, but if I don't come back, Conrad said he'll report me to the police. He wants to discover who stole um...something from him."

"He's blackmailing you? And you want to remain involved with this family?"

I peered through a crack in the wooden door to see her father dressed in black with a white collar – confirming he was indeed the vicar. Grace was standing next to the old horse, rubbing its head.

"Working in the public house was bad enough," the vicar continued. "Cavorting with Doyle is another thing. But staying here overnight? I'd go in there myself and demand Robert Doyle marries you if they were not such a disagreeable family."

"Robert is nothing like his father," she said. "And please do not fuss. I've been allocated my own room."

"You think I'm stupid? Your mother's so embarrassed. There we are every Sunday preaching to the community about family values and our very own daughter is acting out in this way. Having relations outside of wedlock. Have you any idea the danger you're putting yourself in?"

"I can't help it if I'm in love with him."

"He'll not marry you."

"I'm going back inside," Grace said. "And you will

have to return home. I'm no longer a child. I'm nearly twenty-five."

"Exactly, you're an old maid and should be settling down to start a family, not giving your best to a man who does not care for you."

"He does care for me." Grace's voice was close and the door swung open.

She tutted as she saw us eavesdropping and stormed away.

We took a slow walk back to Hamilton as the vicar strode passed us, his face crimson.

"What did you make of that?" Lottie asked me, watching the vicar walk away.

"Neither of the parents approve of the pairing. It would be enough to push them away from Dulverton."

"You think they plan to run away and will fund their lives with the proceeds from selling the amulet?" Hamilton asked as I took Prince's leash from him.

"Maybe it's their ticket to India," Lottie said.

"It was only the one ticket," I pointed out. "Not a pair."

"And Robert has an alibi," Lottie said. "But I guess if they were working as a team..."

"I can't see Grace stabbing Shaw," Hamilton added, but he always viewed women in a fairer light.

As we rounded the corner of the house, it was to find a commotion. Freddie was sprawled on the ground, her green dress covered in dirt. Conrad was attempting to lift her up.

We rushed over as Prince barked, pulling on his leash.

"Father, get off of me. You idiotic man." She nearly kicked Conrad with her right foot, the sole dark with dirt.

I baulked at the thought of someone insulting and abusing their parent in such a way. There was really no excuse. I shook my head. Was this someone who would steal from their parent? Could she have also stabbed a man? Staring into her fiery eyes as she noticed me, I decided that I would keep a close eye on Freddie, who was now clutching her left ankle.

"If you wore shoes, it would help," Conrad grumbled.

"I've twisted it," she said to Hamilton. Her demeanour changing as she gazed at him. He approached her as the naturally gallant man he was, and she lifted her hand so he was able to hoist her up.

"Typical for me to trip after the doctor has left," she said, hanging onto his arm.

"Would you like me to look at it?" I asked in a clipped voice, unable to shake off my disapproval.

"I've only twisted it. I simply need help getting to my room." She looked at Hamilton. "So I can remove my dirty dress." She smiled at him.

Hamilton looked utterly shocked.

"I'll help you change," Lottie said quickly.

Lottie and Hamilton assisted Freddie as she hobbled towards the front door. I assumed Lottie was peeved at this distraction, for she was desperate to get away to Tiverton and place the call to Denham Hall. I was left with Conrad as Prince settled at my feet.

"My children," he said, "have no respect. I guess I've never earned it from them, being a total failure." He sighed. "The past few days have been reflective for me. From their point of view, I bet they ask the heavens every day why their mother had to die and not me."

"Conrad," I said, using his Christian name for the first time. "I'm sure they indeed question why their mother was taken from them, I do the same about my late husband, but I'm sure they would not wish you, their father, dead." I was not completely sure of that but wanted to lighten his mood. "You are far from a failure. I was in awe of your artwork. I truly meant it when I said you were gifted."

He sighed. "I should have stuck to the art. My parents were more interested in me entering the mines and starting a family. That's why I travelled south. They were disappointed in me, being an artist." He laughed. "They were of course very pleased when I married Winnie, but I was so angry back then. I couldn't bear to see their faces, knowing I'd given up my art for her, so I banned them from the wedding and haven't seen my blood family since." He sighed. "I don't know if they're alive or dead." As he looked at me, I witnessed acute sadness. "I feel I've isolated myself. It's all my own doing."

I remained silent, taking this information in. "It must have been hard. Giving up your passion and your family in the north."

"I was truly happy when I was painting."

We began a slow walk back to the house. "I'm taking the case seriously," I assured him, feeling for the first time that I wanted to genuinely assist the fellow.

"I'm glad about that, Ellen. First thing, Robert crossed the bridge on foot and went into town with a telegram to instruct my agent to cancel the attendees. They hopefully will not appear; it would be extremely embarrassing. I hope you can get to the bottom of this."

"I intend to find out exactly what happened," I said.

As we entered the house, Hamilton was descending the stairs.

"Lottie's helping Freddie change and said she will meet you in the drawing room when she has finished."

Prince whined.

"I'll take Prince for a quick run if you like?" he said.

I nodded as Conrad sloped off in the direction of his study.

Inside the drawing room, I found Ivy dusting. "I hear you are travelling to Tiverton today?" she said.

"Yes," I replied with a smile. "We've been delayed for a few minutes. Did you hear the commotion? Freddie twisted her ankle and fell."

"She needs a good pair of boots that one. Carrying on like that! And accusing me of killing her mother?" She dusted the mantelpiece clock. "Winnie was an angel to me. It was her that offered me the job here, not Conrad. Although he's been good to Joseph, I can't fault him as far as that's concerned." She faced me. "Joseph confessed to me he's been in that art room." She shook her head. "And that someone has tried to frame him. Conrad spoke to him earlier today. My son is a gentle man. But at least Conrad knows full well it was not him. Joseph has nothing to worry about."

As the subject had been brought up, I decided to confront her. "Maybe Joseph was not pleased that Conrad had taken advantage of his mother? After all, he must have seen the painting of you in the attic and decided to keep it under a cloth."

Ivy swallowed and sat down on the settee, fiddling with her duster. "Neither of them mentioned it to me." She paused. "It's up there?" she asked in a whisper. "He kept it?"

I nodded, assuming Joseph did not tell his mother as he was embarrassed. "So Joseph and Conrad have a close relationship?" I asked.

She nodded. "Conrad spent a lot of time with him as a child, while Freddie and Robert were at school. I guess he missed them." She looked up. "With Conrad coming from the working classes, there was pressure from the Firth family to educate them, for them to be considered middle class. They wanted them to be academic." She sighed. "My Joseph was more interested in practical things, as Conrad is." She smiled, flashing her gapped smile and giving me a flashback to the painting I saw of her.

"What happened between you and Conrad?" I asked quickly.

Ivy looked at me. "What did he say?"

"That he painted you whilst Winnie was away."

"Oh." She sat up in the chair. "Yes." She shook her head. "I felt terrible."

"Did she ever find out?" I asked.

Ivy shook her head. "She never knew." She stood up. "If you will excuse me, now the bridge is open, I'm going out for supplies."

Ivy left the room and I sat for a moment, alone looking around at the comfortable surrounding, imagining it as a once happy home with the sun streaming in. Wondering how the Firths lived, the family who built the house. What would they make of what had happened? After a few minutes had passed I stood up, deciding to take a stroll to find Hamilton and Prince as I assumed Lottie would be ready soon.

Outside, I saw no sign of them as I walked into the garden but sighed inwardly as I found Purnell leaning against a tree. I could not avoid the man as he had clearly spotted me and was grinning in my direction.

He stood up straight as I reached him. "Are you still interviewing and collecting evidence for your amateur investigation?"

"Stop mocking me," I said.

He laughed. "I'm merely taking an interest, considering Conrad has me under house arrest."

"You are under no real obligation to stay. Why don't you leave?" I asked. "A man of your position does not have to abide by a rule set by Conrad Doyle."

"He's asked me to stay." He laughed. "I'd like to think it's because he likes me but I rather guess he's hoping the amulet turns up and that I'll be purchasing it. So what do you deduce?" he asked me.

"You will be updated when it is fitting," I said.

Purnell laughed. "You have nothing, have you? You're missing things that are right in front of your face."

"Like what?" I asked.

"If you need to ask, you're far from the excellent sleuth you make yourself out to be."

"I've never referred to myself in such a way."

He gestured behind him. "Luckily for you the bridge is fixed. You might make it back to Denham Hall in time for a late luncheon, and you can catch up on the gossip with your old school friend."

"I never told you that Lady Denham was my school friend," I said. "How do you know?"

"Because I can read people," he said staring at me and leaning back against the tree.

Can he really read my mind? I thought. The man certainly seemed to know things I had never told him. Then I took a step back. He'd probably asked Lottie. She seemed to find him a friendly chap and had no doubt succumbed to his charming questioning.

"I know a lot about you. I also know you're no sleuth. You're a lady who loves to gossip." He smiled at me. "But don't worry, you'll be returning shortly to your life of luxury."

I felt a rage bubble inside. "I'm going nowhere until the amulet is found!"

Purnell laughed and in that moment, I wanted it to be him – that he had somehow masterminded this theft and was framing poor Joseph. Every part of me wanted to leave Moor House but the sight of Purnell's smirking face enraged me. I felt the need to prove him wrong.

His expression changed and I guess my heated face and focused stare had given him the message that I was far from pleased with him.

He stood up straight. "I apologise most sincerely, Lady Ellen. I've taken things too far." He sounded sincere and the usual laughter was absent from his eyes.

I took a deep breath and crossed my arms.

"I have been most ungallant for my own amusement and I insulted you." He paused. "I must admit, I enjoy your company and I've put my own need to be in your presence over common decency. But I can assure you I never stole the piece." He turned around to make sure no one else was in the vicinity. "I'll be honest, I didn't like the object and have no intention of honouring my bid if it's found."

"So why are you taking an interest?" I hissed at him.

"Same as you." He shrugged. "I love a mystery." He took a step towards me and looked at me intently. "Anything enigmatic draws me in."

I felt my cheeks flush. I wished I had never set eyes upon Lord Purnell. But this was an opportunity to interrogate the fellow. I uncrossed my arms and attempted to relax. "You are an obvious suspect. You turn up early before the other bidders arrive. A mysterious guest?"

He took another step forward. "You find me mysterious, do you?" He had a twinkle in his eye.

"Please, Lord Purnell. I'm afraid that your excessive flirtation is unwanted."

Purnell grabbed my hand.

Shocked, I gasped. For one moment I thought he was to hurt me.

As if sensing I might scream, he put his finger to his lips. "Shhh. Someone's coming." He did not let go of my hand and led me further into the woods. We stopped and stood behind a tree.

I pulled my hand away from his.

I heard a twig snap and looked around to see Grace and Robert pass us.

"That looks interesting," Grace said as she walked by, clearly peeved that she had caught me eavesdropping on the argument with her father. They carried on into the wood.

I shook my head at Purnell. "You're putting me in a compromising position," I said with my hands on my hips. It was something I seemed to do a lot in his presence. It was not a stance I usually adopted.

"I wish I really were putting you in a compromising position," he said in a low voice.

"Really," I said as I stepped aside. "I need to return to the house as I am taking a trip."

"Am I able to join you?" he asked.

"No!" I could not believe the gall of the man. "I will no doubt see you at dinner."

"Good luck," Purnell said as he went in the direction that Robert and Grace had taken.

I hoped that Lottie was now free for our trip to Tiverton. I felt more than ever that I had to get away.

Chapter Twenty

Even though it was a pleasant day, with the unseasonable weather we had been experiencing, I did not want to get caught in rain and had kept the roof in place on the motorcar. With Prince asleep on the back seat, Lottie sat beside me, with worry etched onto her young face. It was usually so bright. I turned to face front and felt awful knowing she was so concerned.

"Lottie," I said, trying to make conversation, "how did you find Freddie?"

"Awful." Lottie's voice was flat and my attempt at engaging her in conversation did not appear to be working.

"I shall place the call to Denham Hall as soon as we arrive in Tiverton."

"Thank you, Ellen," she said with a small voice. "I'm sorry to be so glum. I worry..." She trailed off.

I felt rather angry with young Sebastian for not communicating with her. It was out of character, but I guessed his family had placed great pressure on him. As I drove over the newly fixed bridge, I held my breath – but the structure was strong and creaked less than when we had arrived. I assumed it had been reinforced after the tree had been removed. We drove alongside the river, and I thought about Hamilton's stick and smiled to myself. I was so pleased that he had moved on, although I felt a slight sense of loss, for it had belonged to my papa. We drove slowly through the town as it was market day and many were out in the small but bustling area, which no doubt brought visitors from across the moor.

I thought of Hamilton as we drove along country lanes. He made me feel calm during investigations. He was a good influence on me, like a rock. Unlike Lord Purnell who left me feeling most uncomfortable. I pushed thoughts of the man from my mind. I hoped that he soon left or that Conrad banished him. But I doubted that would happen. Conrad wanted him to stay, to accept his decent yet false offer. I felt conflicted as I thought I really should divulge to Conrad what Purnell had told me. He would surely banish him, but as he remained on my suspect list, I was compelled to endure the fellow until the mystery was solved. *If I solve it,* I thought, doubting myself.

Once we reached Tiverton, I parked the motorcar and we alighted, heading for the post office where I hoped to find a public call office. I tied Prince to a lamppost outside.

Inside we were in luck and were directed to the telephone. I sat with Lottie by my side and was soon speaking to my best friend.

"Ellen, I was fraught with worry. I placed a call through to a friend near Dulverton who told me all about the bridge and that Moor House had been cut off. Will you soon be back?"

I explained to Phoebe about the theft.

"You have a life filled with excitement. If I did not have the girls I would rush over!"

"Have you had any letters forwarded for us?" I asked Phoebe as I looked at Lottie's expectant face.

"I'm afraid not," she said. "Nothing from Lord Garthorn."

I looked at Lottie and shook my head. She pulled a handkerchief from her pocket.

"When are you returning?" Phoebe asked.

"As soon as we discover what happened to the amulet," I said.

After ending the call I comforted Lottie. My heart

burned for the girl. "I'm so sorry. I will call through to Millar's Hotel and The Grand."

After calling both Branden Bay hotels, it transpired there was no word from Sebastian.

Lottie failed to hold back the tears which now streamed down her face. "I've lost him," she whispered then put her head into her hands. "I was never going to be good enough."

I placed my arm around her. "I'm sure he has an explanation and will be back in England next month as he's due to start at Oxford University."

She wiped her eyes with a handkerchief and sniffed. "I think I have to accept – I'll never see him again." She descended into sobs.

After I had paid for the calls, I took Lottie's hand. "Let's go to a tearoom," I said, hoping a very sweet cake would ease her mood.

Having retrieved Prince, we strolled along the bustling street of the quaint town and stopped for a light lunch at a café in a side street off Fore Street. It had turned out to be a rather warm and sunny day. The cosy establishment had a handful of small tables inside as well as a couple set up outside under the shade of a striped awning. Considering we had Prince with us, we opted to dine al fresco. A crisp white linen cloth covered the tabletop and as we took our seats, a gentle breeze provided relief from the midday heat. It was lovely for me to sit there, remaining anonymous. If I were to take a seat on the street in Ashcombe, I would surely be unable to sit without interruption.

The café's chalkboard menu listed typical fare for light meals. I was rather famished and ordered a Ploughman's lunch, which arrived with thick slices of crusty bread, a hunk of tangy Cheddar cheese, some sticky Huntsman pickle and a few wedges of apple. A small dish of fresh radishes added a peppery crunch. I encouraged Lottie to eat and watched as she chewed slowly, her cheeks stained with tears. She was depicting the epitome of a broken heart. I indulged in an elegant Victoria sponge filled with sweet strawberry jam and whipped cream, which I noted she managed to also devour. Lottie had fallen silent so I listened to the hum of conversation and laughter around us. Once finished, I asked the owner where the closest open area was so we could give Prince a run before we headed back to Moor House.

As we walked back along Fore Street, I glanced into the shop windows displaying their wares. I bought a national newspaper for Hamilton as I knew he liked to keep up with current affairs. We came to a jeweller and I noticed an eye-catching sapphire ring. I stopped in my tracks as Prince tugged on his leash, eager for a run.

"Take Prince," I said to Lottie.

"What's wrong?" she asked as she took the leash from me.

"That ring." I put my hand up to my mouth. "It resembles one Freddie told me about." I felt breathless. I was close, I knew it. "I'm going in," I said.

Lottie nodded at me and then stared at the ring.

The entrance was locked, but there was a bell. I rang it.

A woman smiled and opened the door. "Is there anything you're interested in?"

I nodded. "Yes, that ring." I gestured towards it. "The sapphire with the setting consisting of stars."

"Ah yes, we've had that for a couple of weeks now. We've had a lot of interest, however it's a rather pricey item."

"It's exquisite," I said. "Please may I try it on?"

The lady stepped to one side so that I was able to enter, then locked the door behind us. "I can't be too careful. Not with that thief, The Magpie, around. Stealing from folks in Dulverton. It's only a matter of time before he goes further afield."

The jeweller fetched the ring and then placed it on a black velvet piece of cloth.

My hand shook as I picked it up and eased it onto my index finger, which I felt would be the best fit for the size.

"It's beautiful," I said breathlessly. "And what's the history of the ring?" I asked as I admired it.

"We can't really divulge where it came from. Many families fall upon hard times and are embarrassed when they have to pass such items on."

I removed the ring and checked the inner rim. It was inscribed with 'Shine Bright'. I knew then for sure that this was the ring Freddie had told me about. The ring her mother had inherited. A ring which was stolen by The Magpie.

I placed it back on the velvet cloth with a shaking hand. "The thing is, Mrs..."

"Knox." She smiled at me.

"Mrs Knox, I'm afraid I have to inform you that this ring has been stolen."

The smile slid from her face. "And what makes you think that?"

"I don't think it, I know it. And it was stolen by The Magpie."

"You know this how?"

"Have you heard of Conrad Doyle?" I asked.

She nodded. "He was the first victim of The Magpie. It was in the Gazette."

"This ring belonged to his late wife."

She shook her head. "It was not The Magpie who brought it in. It was a woman. A lovely woman who said she had to sell it to pay for a trip she was taking."

"And who was this woman?" I asked as my heart thudded.

"As I said, I can't divulge..."

"I've been appointed by Conrad Doyle to investigate the matter. It won't reflect well on your business," I said. "Receiving and selling stolen goods."

"But...I..." she stuttered.

"How much did you pay for the item?" I asked, reaching for my purse. "I would not wish you to be left out of pocket.

"Twenty pounds," she said. "But I was going to sell it for forty, it's a large stone."

"Here. I will buy it from you, but I will only compensate you for the money you paid. But you must tell me. What did the woman who sold it to you look like?"

"She was blonde," Mrs Knox said clearly put out that she was not going to make a profit on the ring.

Grace? I thought. Maybe Conrad had been right.

"She was ever so very friendly and had a big smile. With a gap between her teeth."

I placed my hand to my mouth. It was not Grace who sold the jewellery on. The thief was Ivy Wood.

Chapter Twenty-One

As soon as we arrived at Moor House, I updated Hamilton whilst he helped us out of the motorcar.

Lottie sighed. "I hope Ivy confesses and we can leave."

"She'll have no other choice, she's quite recognisable," Hamilton said.

"After we discuss it with her, we'll pass all the details to the police and be on our way to Denham," I said.

"We should have gone to the police first," Lottie grumbled.

"I feel we owe the woman the chance to prepare," Hamilton said. "To compose herself for she is sadly about to be put behind bars. I will ensure she makes no escape. It appears the theft of the Doyle family jewellery was not by The Magpie at all. I say," Hamilton stopped dead. "I've had a thought."

"About what?" Lottie asked.

"The fact that Shaw was asleep during the attack."

"Ah, why did I not think of that? I must be losing my touch!" I said.

"What do you mean?" Lottie asked.

"Shaw fell asleep," I said. "The last thing he drank beforehand was the lemonade Ivy took up for him."

"So he could have fallen asleep because he was drugged, rather than tired?" she said with her eyes wide open.

"We need to tread carefully," Hamilton said. "This is a calculating woman who may already have planned her escape and could cause us harm."

"Too bad for her that we've located and hidden her one-way ticket." I felt my nerves heighten as we walked through the house towards the kitchen.

Ivy looked up from her food prep as we entered. "Did you have a nice day?" she asked as if she was the kindest woman on earth.

How can she act so cool, with what she has done? With that thought I did not return her smile and reached into my handbag. "I've something to show you," I said. I thought I would give her the opportunity to confess, rather than accuse her.

I placed the box on the table before her, then lifted the lid to reveal the ring.

She stared at it, her jaw dropping, then she looked up at me with panic in her eyes. “It looks just like a ring which belonged to Mrs Doyle, bless her soul.” She visibly gulped. “Where did you get it?”

“That’s the question I was about to ask you,” I said. “I know who the ring belonged to and that it was stolen from this house and that you sold it to a jeweller in Tiverton for twenty pounds.”

Ivy put her paring knife down and placed her palms on the table. “I never stole it, it wasn’t me. I found it with some other pieces. Conrad owes me weeks of unpaid wages. It was a way to get the money I deserved.”

I sighed. I’d been hoping she would simply confess. I should have realised it wouldn’t be that easy. “Where did you find it?” I asked.

“In the barn. I can show you.” She stood up. “Someone else stole it.”

“Why didn’t you inform Conrad?” I asked.

“I was angry with him.” She shrugged. “I saw it as my way out.”

“So you bought a ticket, to escape this place?” Hamilton said.

“How do you know that?” she asked with a frown.

"We found the ticket," Lottie said. "We have it so don't think about leaving town."

"Don't you judge me. I've been living here for years under the same roof as the man I love, unable to be with him. I don't care about his stupid amulet." She burst into tears. "He wants someone rich." She gestured at me. "Like you! How can I remain here, to be rejected all over again?"

"I can assure you Mrs Wood, I have no designs on Conrad Doyle," I said.

She hiccupped. "I have to face facts. He doesn't love me. I will find a new life elsewhere."

"And what about Joseph?" I asked.

"He thinks Conrad can do no wrong." She shook her head.

"Would you show us where you found the ring, Mrs Wood?" Hamilton asked, trying to calm the woman down. I frowned at him. Was Hamilton already being drawn in by her?

Ivy took a deep, shuddery breath. "Of course. I've known for weeks. It wasn't The Magpie who stole Winnie's jewellery, it was someone in this house."

"Who?" I asked.

"I've no idea and I really don't care. I'll be leaving as soon as possible," she said. "As long as you return the ticket you say you've taken from me!"

"A ticket bought using stolen goods?" I said, realising it must have been more than the one ring she sold to buy the ticket to India.

Ivy made no comment as she walked out of the kitchen and we followed her to the servant's entrance and then into the barn.

"Over there," she said pointing to the corner. The horse had since been moved.

Hamilton approached a small haystack and dug around with particles rising into the air from the pile. He soon pulled out a box and lifted the lid. "Quite a bounty in here. Mrs Doyle had much jewellery," he said.

I walked over and stood beside him. Amongst the various items I spotting a pearl necklace, I reached forward and lifted it up. On the clasp were the initials DM. *Delia Monroe, the second victim,* I thought as a realisation seeped through me as I stepped back and looked again at the haystack. "What's that?" I said. "There is something else there." I pointed to a black handle poking out from the hay.

Hamilton put his hand back in and pulled out a black bag. Lifting it up, he opened it and pulled out a set of black clothes. A woollen hat fell to the floor, confirming what I had feared.

"Is that the disguise used to pretend to be The Magpie?" Lottie asked.

"It's not me," Ivy said in a panicked voice. "I just

found the jewellery and saw it as my way out! And I never saw that other bag neither, with the clothes in."

I pointed to the box. "Did you not realise that this contains jewellery belonging to many people?"

She shook her head. "No! I recognised the things belonging to Winnie and thought the rest were family heirlooms she never wore."

"I can't see the amulet here," Hamilton said, fishing through the jewellery.

Conrad appeared in the door. "What's going on in here?"

Ivy burst into tears and ran out, pushing by him.

Conrad stared at the box. "Winnie's jewellery?" He went over to the box and lifted a bracelet. "This is not all hers." He looked at me.

I nodded. "I thought Shaw was stabbed by someone who was *pretending* to be The Magpie. But I now fear The Magpie resides in this house."

All the inhabitants of the house had been called yet again to the drawing room. Ivy was missing, she had refused to join us.

"We are going to have this out once and for all," Conrad said. His face was so red I was worried for the man's health. He had gone past the place where a cigarette could calm him and held a large tumbler of whisky in his hand. "You have to tell the truth." He placed the glass on the mantelpiece and grabbed a fistful of jewellery from the box Hamilton held. "Which one of you is The Magpie?"

Freddie sat with her bandaged foot elevated on a table. Her mouth wide open. "Is the sapphire ring there?" she asked.

"It was," I said and passed her the box in which it was nestled.

Freddie's eyes misted over. "Thank you so much." She removed the ring and pushed it onto her finger. "It means so much." Then she scanned the room, her eyes wild. "Which one of you stole Mother's jewellery?"

No one replied and Conrad took another gulp of his whisky.

"I said which one of you was it?" Freddie demanded.

Grace began to cry from across the room.

Robert shook his head at her.

"You?" Conrad stepped away from the fireplace.

"No, Father," Robert said as he stood up. "It is me. I'm The Magpie."

Purnell laughed. "Well I never!"

"What?" Conrad said with a gasp. "My own son?" He grabbed his glass from the mantelpiece and took another mouthful of whisky. He choked on it and we all watched in silence as he composed himself.

"You stabbed Shaw?" Freddie asked Robert aghast, gesturing at the butler.

Shaw stared on in silence as Joseph placed a comforting hand upon his shoulder. I felt for the man. He had been hurt, not just physically, but I presumed he was also hurting on the inside, having been assaulted so horrifically by someone he had known for many years.

"Of course he didn't hurt Shaw," Grace cried. "He's not taken that amulet."

"I bet you put him up to this!" Conrad said pointing at her. "You're a dreadful woman, the spawn of the devil and you have turned my son against me!" His eyes bulged.

Grace put her head down and sobbed with her hands to her face.

Lottie grabbed my hand from beside me as we watched on.

"Father, it was nothing to do with Grace." Robert's eyes were wild.

"But why?" Conrad asked, looking at him in disbelief.

Robert hung his head and said nothing.

"This is out of our hands now," I said. "It is not only your late wife's jewellery contained in the box."

"I will fetch the policeman from Dulverton,"

Hamilton said, placing the box of jewellery on the coffee table.

"No," Robert said. "I will go of my own free will. You can accompany me there." He sloped out of the room and then Hamilton followed with the jewellery.

"How could he?" Conrad asked in a near whisper as Freddie limped across the room and placed a comforting arm around him. "My own son a renowned thief – what have I bred?" Conrad said. "He must have taken the amulet."

Chapter Twenty-Two

"He's still denying selling the amulet," Conrad said over breakfast the following morning. We had all retired early the previous evening, after the revelation. I certainly felt we needed to give Conrad and Freddie some space. Hopefully, as awful as this situation was, it would bring the father and daughter closer together. She was seated next to him at the table. Conrad appeared to be off his food as he was only drinking tea.

"It's most curious," I said as I moved scrambled egg about my plate, finding also that my appetite had left me. How awful it must feel to be betrayed by your own family..."

"We need a thorough search of the house," Conrad said. "The amulet is here, I know it."

Shaw stood up. He was now strong enough to be

out of bed and Conrad had asked him to spend breakfast with him, considering the evidence suggested his son had stabbed the poor man, even though Robert had denied it. "Am I permitted to return to my cottage?" Shaw asked.

"No. I need everyone's help and you can man the front door and alert me to any visitors," Conrad said. "I know Robert did you wrong, but we need to locate the amulet before the police arrive and turn the whole house upside down. I've no idea if Robert or Doctor Jones will now mention that you were stabbed."

"I'm not reporting it," Shaw said. "I will only be left with a scar and have no wish to be interrogated by Sergeant Owens." He sighed. "As much as Robert has hurt me, I will not press charges."

"If they find out they'll probably assign a detective. I don't want anyone interfering." Conrad shook his head and I had to wonder whether he had other business dealings which were not entirely above board.

Freddie shook her head. "My brother, a thief? Stealing Mother's things? I can't bear it here any longer and if he's released I will not be sharing this house with him."

"I doubt he'll be back," Conrad said. "He's not welcome."

"This bacon is divine," Lord Purnell said to Ivy as she entered the room and quietly collected Freddie and Shaw's plates. "There's nothing better than starting the day with a hearty breakfast." He lifted the cloche and took out another thick slice as if it was a normal day.

"I would like to visit Grace," I said.

"I heard the police have questioned her about being an accomplice," Ivy said. "Sergeant Owens let her go as Robert's told him she had nothing to do with it, She's back at the vicarage."

I had a feeling Robert was protecting her. I was sure she must have known about the jewellery judging by her reaction when he confessed.

I stood up. "If you will excuse me, I'll visit her and ask about the amulet. Come along Lottie. She likes you and is more likely to tell the truth if you're there."

"I can't believe my own flesh and blood has done this to me," Conrad repeated as he had done numerous times that morning.

"I'll be honest, I'm surprised he was that agile," Purnell said as we were leaving. "Bit of a podgy chap."

I stopped and turned to face him. "Please, Lord Purnell, there is no need to be rude." I shook my head, wondering why on earth the man was still there.

"I'm simply voicing my opinion. And it's true, isn't it? He was the last person I thought was The Magpie. Did you check the outfit even fitted him?" He raised his eyebrows at me.

"It's not Cinderella and her glass slipper," Lottie said, seemingly tiring of Purnell.

Although I had to admit, Purnell did have a point. "Come along Lottie," I said. "Prince will be restless."

We decided to walk into Dulverton, rather than take the motorcar. As we wandered along the road, we passed Shaw's cottage. I had forgotten the key, otherwise I would have replaced it. I needed to do that before Shaw returned. From Conrad's reaction, I was dismissing the idea that the theft was an elaborate ruse to enable Conrad to stab Shaw and get away with it. My mind had been erratic and I had been finding it hard to focus. It was probably due to being trapped in the house. I had reached the conclusion that Conrad had no knowledge of his wife's indiscretion and if he did, he was in no place to judge considering his dalliance with Ivy Wood.

The walk was a pleasant one, since the summer weather had returned after the deluge. We took a footpath through the woods along the far side of the river, following the line of the water through established woods along a well-trodden path through the soft forest floor. Prince was in and out of the bushes and much happier than when cooped up in the scullery. As we finally dropped into Dulverton, we headed for the church where I expected to find Grace. I needed to understand Robert's motives and whether or not he did have the amulet and was clutching onto it, hoping it would not be discovered. I would have to rely on my own senses to tell whether the girl was being truthful or not.

When we reached the church, we found the door open and I spotted Grace sitting on a pew some way from the altar. She turned as we entered then faced the altar again, her shoulders shaking, telling me she was sobbing. I sensed immediately that this was a woman wanting to confess. I took a seat beside her whilst Lottie remained at the back with Prince.

I placed a hand upon Grace's shoulder. "Shall we go to the vestry and talk?" I whispered. There were a couple of other people in the church absorbed in private prayer.

Grace nodded. I turned and gestured to Lottie to follow us.

Once we were in the vestry, Grace paced the room which consisted of a pew and hooks upon which robes were hung. "I don't know what to do. I can't leave Robert in there taking all of the blame."

"Were you his accomplice?" Lottie asked, wide-eyed, as she settled Prince down.

"Sitting in front of the altar this morning, I realised I need to tell the truth. Then you walked in, as if you were sent by the Lord himself." She sighed. "Even though I've fought against the upbringing I had, I still have a sense of right and wrong. I cannot let someone else take the blame."

I thought back to the clothes we had found and then remembered the bulk of Robert Doyle, which Lord Purnell had so rudely pointed out.

I blinked as I stared at her. "You're The Magpie?" I asked in a whisper.

"What?" Lottie said aghast and Prince barked, creating an echo in the stone walled and floored room. "Shhh, Prince!" She rubbed his back.

Grace nodded then sobbed into her handkerchief. "Robert found me with the jewellery and blamed himself. He said if he was independently wealthy, he could have taken care of me and that I would not have been led to such extremes to make money." She sighed. "The thing is, I didn't do it for the money." She plonked herself on the wooden pew. "Yes, I stole the family jewellery after Conrad had sacked me. It was to get back at him. To hurt him as I was so angry. But I hid it in the barn and never removed it from the property." She shook her head. "To be honest, I enjoyed the excitement of stealing it. It was thrilling, concealing myself in the house and then waiting for them all to go to sleep. And then Delia Monroe, the grocer's wife, was rude to me at the inn, so I got my own back by taking her pearl necklace. And then another customer accused me of giving him the wrong change, so that night I took his watch and another few items from his cottage." She swallowed. "When they named me *The Magpie,* I'm ashamed to admit, it went right to my head." She ran a hand though her bobbed hair. "I was going to give it all back, honestly. I'd planned it out. To return it one night and then listen to everyone chatting about it." She looked up. "When Robert found out, he told me it had to stop and that he would make enough money so we could be together."

I nodded. "So he stole the amulet?"

"No!" She shook her head. "He said he would take over the business from his father and do a much better job. He's been making contacts and has planned a trip to Egypt and was supposed to be taking me too, after we wed in private." She stopped and swallowed. "I can't go now." She gave a shuddery inward breath. "Or get married." She looked down at her hands. "We were going to move to Exeter, which is a much better place to base the business than Dulverton. Then his stupid father lost everything, spending his remaining money and emptying the business account buying that amulet." She looked into my eyes. "I've not even set eyes on the piece, let alone stolen it. When I said it wasn't The Magpie that took the amulet, it was the truth. It wasn't me and Robert was in the barn with me at the time of the theft."

Lottie frowned at her. I assumed Grace was setting

Robert up with an alibi and was lying. I did not challenge her, but noted I could not trust her.

"And what do you intend to do now?" I asked gently.

"I'm going to tell Sergeant Owens the truth," she said then exhaled. "Robert's still here, Owens hasn't transferred him to Tiverton yet."

"Robert will still be in trouble for not bringing the matter to their attention." I stood up. "But it's a brave thing you are about to do."

Lottie and I left Grace and took the road back to Moor House. The river was high, thanks to the rain we'd had. The sound of the babbling water had a calming effect on me as we strolled along, listening also to the birds in the trees which rustled with the occasional breeze.

As we finally reached the house, Hamilton approached us.

"Did you speak to Grace?" he asked.

I nodded. "She says that it wasn't Robert who stole the amulet, and he's not The Magpie." I brought him up to date.

"And you believe Grace? She's not sacrificing herself for the man she loves and hiding the fact they have a priceless item hidden somewhere in the house?"

"I do not trust them. She gave us a false alibi for Robert, saying he was in the barn at the time of the theft when we know he was with Conrad as Lottie heard him."

"Why would she do that?" Hamilton asked.

"To give herself an alibi," Lottie said. "If they did steal the amulet, she can't sell it. It would be better for her to be in prison while he sells it and then when she gets out they can run away together."

"You make a good point," I said to Lottie.

"Something else important to report," Hamilton said. "The newspaper you bought me yesterday in Tiverton describes an amulet which was stolen whilst in transit from Egypt to the British Museum. It's part of a much larger piece and is priceless, apparently. From the head of an elaborately carved sphinx. It was gouged out. And the sphinx is of much significance, having lain in an inner tomb. There's a picture in the paper, which I have left with Conrad. There is little doubt that it's the amulet he bought from Donny Fingo."

"Oh no," I said, "So it was stolen after all? How's Conrad taking that?"

He shook his head. "The man is locked in his study with a bottle of whisky. Whether or not the amulet is found, he realises he cannot keep and profit from it. It will have to be returned to the British Museum. And he's dealing with the knowledge that his funds have run dry. When word gets out that he touched that amulet, no one will buy anything from the man, or Robert."

"I'm beginning to feel sorry for him," Lottie said.

"He's worried that if it's not found and returned he could be implicated," Hamilton said. "Therefore he's still as keen for us to search for the item."

"What a mess," Lottie said.

"Moor House may have to be sold," Hamilton said.

"And the Fingo brothers aren't able to take the heat, considering the Vigilante Slasher killed them both!" Lottie added.

"No," Hamilton said with a grim shake of his head. "It's most unfortunate." He took a deep breath. "What do you want to do next, Ellen? Conrad has all available hands searching the house for the amulet. They've started in the bedrooms and will leave the barn until the end, with it being a messy job."

"I wish to revisit the scene of the crime," I said. "It often helps, doesn't it? To see and imagine what happened. I've information swirling around my head and without a notebook, it's simply jumbled and I can't make sense of it."

"We'll go up to the attic now," Lottie said eagerly. "I want to get it solved and away from this house as soon as possible. It looked so peaceful and pretty when we arrived."

We fed Prince then left him once he settled in the

scullery. We walked through the house and up both flights to the attic room where Shaw had been guarding the amulet. I pulled the chair back to the centre of the room, where the butler had been sitting, and gestured to Lottie. "Sit in the seat, you will play Shaw." I gestured to Hamilton. "And Ernest, you can play the part of the thief." I completely opened the window. It had been partially open as the fire rope remained where it had previously been dropped. I turned to face the pair. "Shaw was asleep, regardless of the manner in which he fell asleep – whether it was tiredness or a drugged glass of lemonade."

Lottie lowered her head as if sleeping.

I frowned at Hamilton. "I doubt the thief came in the window, especially in the rain. They would have been spotted during daylight scaling the roof, and there would have been wet footprints. The roof would have been slippery." I looked to my left. "He or she must have come through the door. Maybe they hid in the art room and crept out when they knew Shaw was alone. We know they used it to hide the amulet, so they must have a copy of the key. But it is curious that no one saw them, not even Ivy when she delivered the lemonade."

"Unless it was her," Lottie said, lifting her head.

I stood beside her. "Move the chair away." I pulled a blanket from a nearby chair and placed it on the floor to protect my clothes from the dried blood stains which were still on the rug, and then laid on the floor, looking at the room from Shaw's perspective. "Stand closer to the window," I said to Hamilton, imagining he was wearing black. "It doesn't make sense." I leaned up on my elbow and as I did, I felt the floorboard beneath me move. I heaved myself up, helped by Hamilton, looked down and pulled back the blanket and then the blood-stained rug to find a loose floorboard. I looked closer and saw a trace of blood. "Hamilton, can you lift this board?"

My heart thumped as Hamilton prised the loose floorboard up with his pocket knife. "Nothing inside here. It's empty," he said.

Whilst that was indeed true, I could see the tell-tale trace of blood within. And slowly, as if a fog was clearing, the clues I had discovered over the preceding days slotted into place.

I gestured at Hamilton. "Can you arrange for everyone to meet us in the drawing room in one hour."

All I needed was to calmly piece it together in an orderly fashion.

Chapter Twenty-Three

An hour later, I entered the drawing room and stopped still. Robert was there.

"Sergeant Owens allowed Robert to return," Hamilton said. "But has kept Grace in custody. He's going through the jewellery with her to ascertain what belongs to whom before he takes the matter forward."

"The woman confessed," Conrad hissed and then gestured at his son. "I told you she's no good for you! A thief on my own staff and you covering up her actions and then taking the blame? She's seduced and over-powered you, my son. What sort of man are you? You had an advanced education. I was brought up working in a pit and am more astute than you!"

"Father, you've made your point." Robert shook his head.

"Lady Ellen wants to address everyone," Conrad slurred, clearly having indulged in too much whisky. "She believes she knows what happened to the amulet and wishes for it to be returned to the British Museum. As do I. I would like to avoid this coming out into the open. As yet, the police are unaware of the situation and only have details of the local jewellery that was stolen. Could you all please give her your full attention."

"I can't wait for this," Purnell said, rubbing his hands together. I was looking forward to the moment I would wipe the doubting smirk from his face.

I stood up to address the room. All apart from Purnell were seated. I took a deep breath and spoke clearly. "I spent a lot of time deliberating, wondering who could have done this atrocious thing, to stab a man without even a struggle. Whilst he sat vulnerable and asleep. Who could be so viscous?"

"Asleep?" Conrad said staring at Shaw.

Shaw lowered his head. "I'm so sorry Mr Doyle. It's true I fell asleep." He looked up.

I continued. "It was a tricky case because as a household you all hold so many secrets."

Conrad's eyes darted to me, then Ivy and finally to Joseph.

"I'm sorry, Mr Doyle, but I'm unable to reveal the truth and go through the various alibis without divulging your truth," I said. "You have been hindering my investigation as much as anyone else. By not telling us that it was Joseph who was with you at the time of the theft – not Robert. That led me to assume that Joseph was the thief, considering his whittling knife was doused in blood and concealed in your art room, which he has been using."

Lottie frowned. "Joseph?" She sat back.

Conrad nodded and looked down at his hands. "Go on."

"Conrad Doyle has spent twenty-four years denying his own flesh and blood," I said.

Robert looked up. "What do you mean?"

Conrad swallowed. "You have a brother," he said with a rasp. "An older brother."

Joseph looked at Conrad, his face showing adoration. I was struck at how little Conrad had to do to gain love and respect from Joseph, compared to his legitimate children.

I continued. "We thought that Robert had an alibi for the theft of the amulet because Lottie heard voices coming from Conrad's study. 'Father, we have to tell the others', and Conrad said 'No, never." She assumed it was Robert speaking to him but of course it was his eldest son, Joseph."

"Joseph?" Robert stood up, staring at his half-brother in disbelief. Then he looked back to Conrad. In the light of that knowledge, there was a visible likeness between Joseph and Conrad. Their height, their noses, their eyebrows. Subtle likenesses one would not necessarily pick up on, with them having such differing colouring. Whereas apart from sharing his father's hair colour, Robert on the other hand clearly looked more like his sister and mother.

Conrad gestured towards Ivy. "Ivy modelled for me in Exeter. We were... She was my fiancée."

"Well I never!" Purnell said.

Shaw frowned, looked at Ivy then back to Conrad, then back down to his hands.

"This explains a lot." Freddie gestured at her father. "You always spent more time with him than us. Now it all makes sense, get rid of us to boarding school whilst the three of you played happy families right under Mother's nose!" She gestured at Ivy. "You killed her, I knew it!"

Ivy pulled a handkerchief from her pocket. "It wasn't like that! I was wronged." She wiped her eyes then looked up at Conrad. "We had plans." She gasped. "You asked me to be your wife!" She forced the words out as tears spilled down her rosy cheeks.

Conrad continued. "Ivy fell pregnant. Whilst she was pregnant and I was trying to figure out how on earth I would be able to support her and a child, I had a weak moment. A time of escapism from my problems. I had a brief affair with a young woman I was commissioned to paint."

"Our mother was an affair?" Robert said and stood up. "Did she know?"

Freddie and Robert both stared at their father, waiting for a response.

"Yes, she knew I was seeing someone, but not who and she had no knowledge that Ivy was expecting a child. Your mother was young and a little wild. Then she too fell pregnant." He ran a hand through his hair.

Hamilton took a sharp intake of breath and shook his head with visible disapproval.

I caught Purnell's eye, who in contrast appeared thoroughly entertained.

"Winnie's father insisted I marry her. He was a fierce man and said he would ruin me. I'm ashamed to admit it." He stopped, clearly fighting his emotions. "I left Ivy and moved here to Dulverton. Choosing a privileged position. I'm a terrible man."

"That we can agree on," Freddie said as she stared at him.

"You were telling the truth," I said to Conrad, "when you said you had not been in the art room since you moved here. The portrait of Ivy was painted before you even arrived at Moor House."

He nodded. "Ivy applied for a position here whilst I was away on business." He gestured to Robert and then Freddie. “Your mother was an angel. She gave Ivy the housekeeping job, even though she had a four-year-old son. As you can imagine, I was shocked to find her here. But Ivy kept our secret, she never told Winnie.”

“And did she find out?” I asked him.

He shook his head. “Not to my knowledge.”

“I never told her,” Ivy said.

“Of course she found out!” Freddie said. “That’s why you pushed her down the slope, into the river.” She gestured at the housekeeper.

“I found her, but I never pushed her,” Ivy said. “I always respected Winnie. I just wanted Joseph to know his father. My needs came second to that.”

“Rubbish,” Freddie said. “Ever since Mother passed, you’ve been after Father.”

Joseph stood up and comforted his mother. He looked neither surprised nor shocked and was clearly aware of his family history.

“How did you find out that Conrad was your father?” I asked Joseph.

“I always considered him to be my father, he brought me up.” He smiled at Conrad. “But he told me himself.”

Conrad shook his head. “I shouldn’t have. I was drunk after one of my parties.”

“There’s a surprise,” Freddie said.

A silence followed and I took a deep breath,

looking around the room before continuing. "The evidence was all pointing at Joseph and it was difficult to ignore. The amulet hidden in the art room he frequented. His knife having been used to stab Shaw and him with no alibi for the time of the crime. Yet it was hard to understand what motive he had, when he loves Moor House. We thought that Robert had an alibi, but it was Joseph with Conrad at the time of the theft." I turned to Robert. "So you had no alibi."

"I never took the amulet. I can assure you. I would have benefitted from the sale Father arranged, although as we now know, it's a piece that was stolen en route to the British Museum." He shook his head at his father.

"The answer to the mystery had been in my hands days ago. But I was thwarted by you, sir." I gestured at Lord Purnell. "You have disrupted and hindered my investigation. If it were not for you, this matter would already have been solved."

"Me?" Purnell said looking genuinely surprised. "I've no part in this affair?"

I continued: "I had deduced when in Shaw's cottage, having found a collection of love letters, that Mrs Winnie Doyle had an affair with a man younger than her years. With her butler."

"What?" Conrad turned to stare at Shaw. "You had an affair with my wife?" His face turned crimson.

"Ivy Wood told me that Shaw had entertained a woman at his cottage and he himself told me that he had known but one love and had not been strong enough to pursue her heart."

"You seduced my wife?" Conrad spluttered. "How could you!"

"I jumped to the wrong conclusion," I said. "Assuming the initial of W referred to Winnie." I turned to look at Conrad's daughter. "When did you find out, Freddie?"

"About what?" she asked.

"That you had a half brother?"

She glowered at me. "Three minutes ago."

"I don't think so. You've known for some time, because the butler sees all." I turned to Shaw. "You knew about Ivy and Conrad's history and it was you who told Freddie."

"I told you in the strictest confidence, man," Conrad said to Shaw. "Why would you?"

Shaw's eyes darted to Freddie and she gave a slight shake of her head, as if to assure him he had nothing to worry about and to keep his mouth closed. But unfortunately for Shaw, he did have a lot to worry about. Freddie narrowed her eyes at me and flared her nostrils.

I was not put off and continued. "I assumed Freddy was short for Frederica."

"It's Winifred," Conrad said. "Same as her Mother. Used to be called by that name until she reinvented herself as Freddie."

Freddie narrowed her eyes at her father.

"Your butler was so in awe of the daughter of his employer, he would do anything for her. She was his first and only love."

"Poor chap," Purnell said with a short laugh.

I ignored his inappropriate comment and continued. "In a locked cupboard in the art room, we found a ticket. We assumed it was Ivy's as she said she had bought a ticket to leave this place. But something nagged at me. Why would a woman who told me as we prepared vegetables together that she hates the heat wish to escape to India?"

"India?" Ivy said. "I was going to Torquay, where my sister and her family live."

I gestured to Freddie. "Unlike Miss Doyle here who is happy to wear a thick dress and a corset on a summer's day without even breaking a sweat."

"Dear me, Lady Ellen, how vulgar of you to mention corset and sweat in the same sentence." Freddie stood up and winced, I presumed from the pain in her ankle. As she gestured at me, her long dress swished about her.

I made no comment. I had become immune to Freddie's taunts, seeing her for who she really was.

"And you have no proof whatsoever to back up your ridiculous lies. You should have stuck to your hospital, or written fiction, as this is completely made up." She glared at me.

"It was one ticket, not a pair." I turned to the butler. "You didn't think she was going to take you with her, did you?"

He stood up. "You were going alone?" He winced, grabbed his wound, then gestured at her. "After all I've done?"

"Sit down you fool!" Freddie shouted at him.

"Can someone please explain what's going on?" Conrad demanded.

"I will," Purnell said. "Shaw —"

"Excuse me, Lord Purnell," I said, facing him yet again with my hands on my hips. There was no way I would allow this man to interrupt. I turned again to address the room. "It was actually Lord Purnell who helped me."

"It was?" Purnell said with amusement.

"He told me he had been reading a book on your bookshelf, which detailed human anatomy. A book that would need to be consulted when deciding where exactly a man should stab himself to avoid any vital organs. It was not luck that the knife missed a fatal strike."

Shaw opened his mouth, then shut it again and

stared at his hands as he wrung them together.

I continued. "Shaw stabbed himself with Joseph's whittling knife, then hid it and the amulet under a loose floorboard in the attic before throwing the fire rope to the floor being sure to wipe his own blood on it, giving the impression The Magpie had left via the window. He then told everyone he'd been attacked by someone resembling The Magpie. When in fact there was never anyone else in the room. He later convinced me that he'd fallen asleep, leading us to wrongly believe that Ivy had drugged him with a laced glass of lemonade." I looked to Shaw. "You were convincing. The stress at the wound you endured was real, when you realised that the doctor and hospital were too far away. Cut off by the fallen tree. I guess Freddie said she would personally drive you to seek medical help."

"This was nothing to do with me! That's totally ridiculous. Tell them Shaw," Freddie said.

"She had nothing to do with it," he said staring at his lap.

"At some point, whilst we were all concerned with Shaw's injuries, Freddie slipped up to the attic, removed the amulet and knife and quickly stored them in a cupboard within the room where her father's art was kept. Should they be found, her half-brother would take the blame, considering Shaw stabbed himself with one of his knives." I turned to Freddie.

"You were wearing a deep red dress that night. One upon which blood was unlikely to show."

Freddie sat staring at me but made no comment.

"I presume she had seen Joseph in there before, and seen the picture of Ivy. Maybe that's when she confided in Shaw, who filled in the missing gaps."

Shaw looked down at his hands as they shook, then back up to Conrad. "Sorry, Conrad."

"You're fired," he spat at him.

"As I said, a man who would do anything for the woman he loves." I turned to Freddie. "Shaw was your first love. And you his."

Freddie laughed. "Preposterous rubbish."

I took a letter from my pocket, which I had retrieved from Shaw's cottage prior to the meeting. "This proves it."

She stared at the butler as if he was a fool for keeping her letters. "Whatever happened when I was younger is irrelevant. I never knew about Joseph being my half brother. You have made incorrect assumptions." She gestured at Shaw "This is a crime he committed himself and had absolutely nothing to do with me."

Now in my stride, I gestured at Freddie in a somewhat unladylike fashion. "You were fed up with scraping by. Of living off the money of the men you despised! And having heard you had an illegitimate older brother, whom you'd always been jealous of, feeling that your father spent more time with him than you, you wanted revenge."

"Are you quite finished?" she asked me.

I continued. "Upon hearing that your father had acquired a priceless object, you decided to steal it and leave the country for a new life. "

"Where the dickens is the amulet?" Conrad demanded.

"Please put us out of our misery, Lady Ellen. Your theatrics must surely be coming to a conclusion," Purnell said. "Although I'm enjoying them immensely."

The thought of Purnell enjoying my speech brought it to a close. "When I first arrived, Freddie unlocked the woodland gate with a key she was keeping about her person." I looked at Freddie and held out my hand. "Please may I have the amulet? You've been wandering around the house for some time with it close to your heart!"

Freddie stood up, faltered, looked around the room and then limped towards the door.

"Freddie, wait," Shaw called.

Hamilton followed her and Purnell made for the door to block her exit, but she instead headed for the door to the dining room to make her escape.

Conrad shouted. "Let her go, that amulet is cursed

and so am I! Nothing I have ever done has worked out. It will bring her bad luck. Look at what happened to the Fingos!"

The others stopped. Shaw followed, calling out to Freddie.

"This whole escapade is a culmination of a lifetime of failure on my part," Conrad said.

"That's not right, Father," Joseph said. "You're an artist. I have savings to get us by. You only need to sell a few paintings a year."

"I'd like to see your art, Father," Robert said as if trying to process everything.

I looked at the dining room door where Freddie had exited. I felt conflicted; the woman was a thief and the amulet needed to be returned to the museum.

We soon heard the sound of a car engine.

Robert went to the window. "Freddie's taken the motorcar! She's left Shaw though."

"The man will have to leave tonight. At least we'll be able to make some money if we find a tenant for his cottage," Conrad said with a sigh.

He turned back to the room and Joseph approached Robert and they shook hands, clearly acknowledging their connection.

"I'll buy one of your paintings," I said to Conrad, struck by the emotion of the moment. "A landscape. I'm redecorating Ashcombe Hall and I'll commission you to paint another of the hall itself when renovations are complete." Why I felt obliged I'd never know. I was still owed the money for his wife's ring which I bought and was now on his fugitive daughter's finger.

"I agree, a landscape is best," Purnell said. "I wouldn't ask him to paint your portrait, you might find yourself with child." He threw his head back and laughed.

The fellow's joke was as usual in bad taste, but it did somewhat lighten the atmosphere, as after a pause Conrad burst into laughter, so hard that he ended up sobbing. It was as if years of untruths had finally caught up with him.

I left the room with Hamilton and Lottie. Purnell followed, leaving the family to start a new life. We stood in the small entrance hall.

"Congratulations, Lady Ellen," Purnell said, with what appeared to be genuine respect.

"How on earth did you arrive at that conclusion?" Hamilton asked.

"When I saw the blood-stained space underneath the floorboard where the knife and possibly the amulet had been hidden, I realised that Shaw had stabbed himself. Then the other clues fell into place." I turned to Purnell. "If I had not been interrupted by you, when I was in Shaw's cottage I would have read the complete letter. When I checked today, I discovered whilst it was a few years old, the letter was clearly from Freddie not her mother. And if we'd had a notebook to see everything clearly, I think we would have solved this matter much sooner."

"We'll have to make sure we buy a notebook next time," Lottie said.

"There will be no next time," I said with a laugh. "I really think it's time we left." Whilst I made no mention of it, I had no intention of Freddie Doyle getting away with the amulet. I knew exactly who to call as soon as we reached Denham.

Hamilton nodded. "If you could possibly drop me at Tiverton station, I have business I must attend to in Bristol."

"It's a shame you can't come to Denham Hall," I said realising we had stayed in Dulverton too long to allow him to make the trip.

"I'm leaving now, also." Purnell said. "It's been interesting. I do hope we will bump into each other again." He took my hand.

I held my breath as he kissed it then I pulled it back. Another meeting with Purnell was the last thing I wished for. "If I'm ever passing Cornwall, I'll be sure to pop by," I said. The county was rather large, but I did not enquire further as to the exact location of his estate, as I had absolutely no intention of meeting the man again.

"Charlotte, Captain Hamilton. It's also been a pleasure." Purnell about-turned and hurried away.

As soon as he was out of the house, Lottie turned to Hamilton. "We're going back to Branden Bay in a week. Will you meet us there?"

Hamilton looked at me as if searching for my permission and as my eyes met his, the thought of spending time with him again in the seaside resort warmed me.

"That would be super," I said, giving him a broad smile and hoping we could spend some special moments together before I returned to my life as lady of the hall. I would have to give up this new world I had been living in, which had fewer barriers. At that moment, I felt there was no barrier between myself and Hamilton.

"We had better pack," he said with a smile. "I will meet you at your car."

Prince barked in the distance and Lottie scurried down the passageway towards the scullery.

There was a knock at the door and Hamilton opened it. It was the postal delivery man and he handed him a letter.

"I'll give this to Conrad and then help you down with your trunk when you are ready."

Whilst Hamilton and Lotte loaded the motorcar, I located Conrad in the drawing room and found him in a much better mood. Indeed, the frown had left his face and he looked so much younger. Even though his daughter and butler had stolen from him, he was in excellent spirits. He passed me a wrapped painting, a gift for the work I had done, which I thanked him for.

"I've got news," Conrad said. "The sergeant has released Grace, since no one has pressed charges. And I'm in no place to judge others. It appears Robert and Grace were planning to wed."

"So what's next for you?" I asked.

"Joseph insists on purchasing some paints and canvases. He's so enthusiastic, I don't want to let him down. And Ivy and I have some soul searching to do."

"I'm sure you won't let anyone down," I said rather hoping he would turn a new leaf.

He lifted the envelope delivered by the postman from the mantelpiece and opened it. "Ah yes, the list of potential bidders for the amulet it must have been held up in transit. Hopefully Freddie will see fit to return it when she comes to her senses." He studied the letter and then frowned. "That's curious, there's no mention at all of a Lord Purnell!" He looked at me. "Who the blazes was the fellow?"

I shrugged. "I don't know and, as long as I don't have to meet the man again, I really don't care."

Chapter Twenty-Four

I headed for Denham Hall. Lottie held the wrapped landscape painting and Prince was in the back. We had dropped Hamilton in Tiverton and I was in good spirits, having arranged to meet him at The Grand Hotel in a week's time.

"I do hope we can relax and enjoy our time here," I called out to Lottie as we took the long drive up to Denham Hall.

"Hmm," Lottie said distantly. I knew that she wanted to find out what had happened to Sebastian and would rather we motored straight to Branden Bay in case he turned up there. But if I had been in need of a rest when I'd left Ashcombe Hall, I was in greater need now and was more likely to find peace and quiet at Phoebe's home than a bustling seaside resort in the height of summer.

As I stopped the engine, it was to find Phoebe waiting for us. I smiled; she always had so much energy and a zest for life. Maybe that was why I has been drawn to Lottie for she also shared Phoebe's youthful outlook.

"I'm so pleased you're back. I cannot wait to hear all about it," she said, grinning at Lottie. "And how are you?"

Lottie gave her a weak smile. "Fine."

Phoebe put an arm around her. "The girls have missed you dreadfully. However, you have competition as they've a new teacher who arrived this morning. A very knowledgeable teacher who they've fallen completely in love with."

"I thought they hated their governesses," I said with surprise.

"Ah, this one is special," she said. "Let me introduce you, they're waiting just inside the door."

The footman took the painting and I collected Prince as Phoebe ushered Lottie inside. I turned around as I heard Lottie cry out, "Sebastian."

Prince woofed and pelted hard, dragging me with him towards the front door. A broad smile crossed my face as we entered to find Sebastian spinning Lottie around in the large reception hall as the twins squealed in delight.

I exchanged a look with Phoebe as they embraced. "It's the modern way," I said.

"It's positively enchanting," Phoebe added. "So much in love!"

"Why did you not write?" Lottie said when he put her down, then pushed him away.

"It's a long story," he said with a hand to his chest.

"Why don't you two go to the garden, and Sebastian can tell you all about it. I'll catch up with Ellen. And girls, up to the nursery and wash your hands for tea." She put her arm in mine. "Now, tell me all about this adventure you've been having."

After we had taken tea and cakes and I had recounted the long story of our latest mystery to Phoebe, she sat back in her chair. "I'd love to meet this Lord Purnell." She frowned. "I have to say, I've never heard of such a fellow."

"I think he was fabricating his title, for when Conrad Doyle received the list of prospective buyers, the man's name was not there."

"Maybe he was on the list, but wanted to remain anonymous, considering the amulet was stolen, and gave a false name."

"Indeed. However you look at it though, he was

clearly a crook." I shuddered. "So what happened with Sebastian?"

"His family announced his engagement without even telling him."

"That's exactly what Hamilton thought had happened."

"It's the families that want to be connected. So old fashioned, but then they are the Marquis and Marchioness of Bandberry. Steeped in tradition." She sighed. "He escaped but had no funds upon him, so had to find his way penniless to Dublin. Once there he had to work to earn enough money to pay for his boat across the sea and then worked in Liverpool to raise the money for his train fare. He finally arrived in Branden Bay to discover Lottie was not there! But managed to get a lift here from someone at Millar's Hotel. A John Breckon, the manager, I believe you spoke of him to me? Stiff man and a little shy but he stayed for a cup of tea before he left."

I smiled, I rather missed Breckon, Norma and even Mrs Flint.

"So how does Lady Bandberry feel about her son absconding?" I asked.

"Sebastian's not contacted her yet. He said he's taking time to think on his future." She lowered her voice. "He's so taken with Lottie. But they are so very young."

"I know and he's off to Oxford next month. I'm sure he'll still attend, he's desperate for the education. And his parents will be relieved when they eventually hear from him. I will urge him to send them a message. They must worry about him, especially as he's their only child."

"Doesn't he know it, so much pressure on the young man. He has a gift for teaching – the girls have learned much from him in only a few hours. Now sit back and relax, Ellen, I want you to promise to stay with me for at least a week before heading back to Branden Bay.

"I'm pleased you said that, as it's the exact length of time I had in mind. Now I really would like to change as I've been wearing the same dresses for days."

* * *

The days sped by. I had placed a call through to Scotland Yard the day we arrived at Denham and asked to speak to Inspector Stone. A policeman I had met during previous cases. He did not sound at all excited to hear from me at the start of the call, but soon mellowed when I gave full details of the theft of the famous and missing amulet and also a description of Freddie Doyle. He had even muttered his thanks. I also made it clear that I had no wish to be linked to the sorry affair and that pleased him even more. I was sure he would be only too happy to capture her and take full credit for returning the amulet to the British Museum.

Lottie and Sebastian had spent much time together. I had insisted that he telephone through to his Mayfair home to leave a message for his parents. I also ensured I kept a watchful eye on the pair. I'd heard enough stories of women finding themselves with child.

The Earl of Denham was due back and I told Phoebe that we would leave once I had taken tea with him, as I had not seen him for some years. Lottie and Sebastian were playing a game with the girls up in their nursery until it was time for us to leave.

"I'm so pleased we've spent some time together," Phoebe said with tears in her eyes. "I do so miss you, so it was lovely to have your company."

Prince woofed from my side.

"And you, boy," she said to him with a laugh.

We heard the sound of an engine and Prince ran to the window.

"Ah, Henry's here. I'll meet him at the motorcar and bring him in and we'll take tea."

She soon returned to the room flushed. "He's brought Alex with him, you'll love him. He's the friend from university, the one I was telling you about – the

Duke of Loxborough. He's passing through on his way to Cornwall following a recent trip to London. He has some sort of undercover job, I think. Tells us his work involves catching bad people." She gestured behind her. "He drove Henry over instead of the chauffeur collecting him." She fanned herself. "As you did not meet him the other week in Exeter, I've invited him in. I hope you don't mind!"

"Of course not." I smiled. I had heard her speak of Alex often and knew she had wanted us to meet for some time. I hesitated. "You're not matchmaking though, are you?"

She put a hand to her chest. "Me? No." She laughed. "I would not do that, considering how taken you are with Captain Hamilton. But I must confess when I met Alex in Exeter, I was rather gossiping about you. I told him all about our time in school together and about your cases in Branden Bay and about the convalescent home and he had already read about you in the newspaper. He does seem rather keen to meet you. So forgive him if he is a little flirtatious."

I felt a little dizzy and held onto the back of a chair.

"Are you quite well?" Phoebe asked me.

Yes," I said, as a spark of intuition hit me.

She bit her lip. "I'm sorry if he appears rather enamoured by you. He's quite a forward chap."

I smiled nervously as I heard the male voices

approaching and a fizzle of recognition hit me. Prince raced towards the door.

First I saw the Earl of Denham enter. "Henry, it's been too long," I said in a light voice, hearing it falter slightly, not wanting to turn my gaze to his friend.

"You haven't aged one bit, Ellen, and it's good to see you out of black." He turned around. "And I must introduce you to an admirer. This is the Duke of Loxborough," he said stepping aside. "Your dod appears to have already introduced himself."

I stared at the Duke of Loxborough with a smile frozen upon my face. Standing before me was of course the man I had come to know as Lord Purnell, he was stroking Prince's head.

He winked at me. I said nothing as he approached and took my hand. "I'm pleased to meet you, at last. My friends call me Alex. Duke is so stuffy."

"Ellen has had another adventure, haven't you?" Phoebe said. "Now come along Henry, the girls are missing you and I've someone to introduce you to. The Marquis of Bandberry's son has called upon us." She looked over to me. "We'll leave Ellen to tell Alex all about her latest adventure." She winked at me and left the room. Phoebe was clearly matchmaking, whether or not she felt I had a connection with Hamilton.

"Would you care to take a turn around the gardens

and tell me all about your adventure," Alex said as he offered me his arm.

I rejected it but accompanied him, in order to tell the man exactly what I thought of his behaviour. I did not want anyone to overhear us. Once we were out of the building, I turned to him.

"What was your intention in Dulverton?" I said.

"I was passing through. Phoebe told me all about you, I was intrigued. I thought I was arriving at a garden party where I could blend in unnoticed and introduce myself. If challenged, I planned to say my car was in need of water. Then Doyle asked if I was there for an auction. And well, I simply went along with it. I'd planned on taking a break in Bath but the trip to Dulverton was just what the doctor ordered." He chuckled.

"So where did the name Purnell come from?"

"It's a brand of cologne."

"Of course," I said. "I knew I'd heard the name somewhere."

"It was the first thing that came to mind." He threw his arm in the air theatrically. "If you smell, use Purnell."

"I don't think that is the exact advertisement," I said.

"My uncle wears it and Conrad Doyle was

drenched in it, so Purnell was the first name that came to mind!" He smiled at me. "I'm always wary of men that smell of too much cologne. Makes me think they don't wash." He gestured around the estate. "Where's your faithful lapdog?"

"I think he's behind that bush," I said and then saw Princes tail wagging from the greenery.

"I meant Captain Ernest Hamilton?"

"He's still in Bristol, I presume." I bristled at his rudeness towards Hamilton, but answered him politely, not wishing to let him see that his words had affected me.

"Bristol you say?" he said with a shake of his head.

The man was already grating on my nerves.

"As I said, you really don't know very much about that man." He stared at me.

"Can we stop this charade?" I said with my hands back on my hips. "You had your fun back in Dulverton."

He smiled at me. "I think you need to set yourself free."

I felt my muscles tense and my lips purse and I took a step backwards.

He threw his head back and laughed. "To the outside world, Ellen, you can come across as quite severe." He paused and regarded me. "But I know a fire burns within you."

I shut my eyes, took a deep breath, then opened them as I exhaled. “If you are quite finished.” I looked him straight in the eye. “I take it we are keeping your alter ego as Lord Purnell quiet from the Denhams?”

“If you wish. It can be our little secret. We need not tell anyone.” He winked at me.

“I do wish.” There was no need for anyone to know. Certainly not Phoebe, who would love that level of gossip, nor Hamilton and Lottie, who would be unlikely to bump into the Duke of Loxborough again.

“Before I go, I have something for you.” He gestured to his car.

I reluctantly followed with Prince now at my side, wondering what it was. He reached inside and pulled out a stick and passed it to me.

“I saw this caught between rocks in Dulverton town. I thought it was Captain Hamilton’s and reached in for it but saw it had your family crest upon it.”

I took the stick and ran my hand over it. Seeing my father’s initials on it plucked at my heartstrings. I had not realised how much the stick had meant to me until it was back in my grasp.

“I had it spruced up. There were a few scratches but it can’t have been in the water for long, else it would have been ruined.”

I gave a genuine smile. “Thank you.”

"It's been fun. Maybe we can do it again some time?"

I made no comment as he gave Prince a final pat on the head. I watched him jump into his car and drive off with a toot of his horn.

Chapter Twenty-Five

I sat in the Richmond room of The Grand Hotel, which was positioned right on the seafront looking out to the promenade. The yellow sands of Branden Bay were crowded with day visitors for it was the weekend and the sun was shining. I had invited John Breckon, Norma Lloyd and Mrs Flint, who I had met at the rival 'Millar's Hotel', to take afternoon tea with myself, Lottie and Sebastian. I was very much looking forward to seeing them and finding out what we had missed whilst away. Hamilton was due in Branden Bay the following day and I had kept it free so we could spend the day together.

Before me was a circular table laid out for six. Lottie and Sebastian had taken Prince for a long walk along to beach so that he would behave himself whilst we enjoyed our tea. I glanced at my wristwatch. I still had fifteen minutes before afternoon tea was due to start. The hotel staff were on hand to fill the table with an array of cakes and pots of tea as soon as my guests arrived. I smiled as I gazed out of the window, appreciating the peace of the room. I felt as if I'd had little time during recent weeks to merely relax and watch the world go by. Which was odd since when Leonard died I had feared loneliness. I had never really experienced it, and coming to Branden Bay for a period of solitude had not resulted in time alone. I smiled as the faces of those people I had met over the previous months floated around my mind.

I glanced around the small private room I had hired. When my guests were here, I did not want our conversation to be overheard. I was certainly interested to hear from them how the new owners of Millar's Hotel were getting along with their planned renovations. I knew they would also wish to hear of our visit to Moor House, which I had delegated to Lottie to tell. I would ensure they were sworn to secrecy.

The door soon swung open. Lottie and Sebastian steamed in with an excited Prince, much earlier than I had expected. *Not even five minutes peace,* I thought with a smile.

Lottie waved a national newspaper at me. "Ellen!"

Prince barked.

I stood up and took my dog's leash. "Shh boy."

Then I looked up at the pair. "Why are you so excited? You're causing Prince to bark. Remember it's the hotel's policy not to allow pets here."

"Apologies, Ellen, but we have news," Sebastian said.

"And what's that?" I asked as I led Prince to the bay window and tried to settle him.

"The Vigilante Slasher has been at work again," Sebastian said.

I spun around and put a hand to my throat. "Really?" I said in a near whisper.

"A woman this time," Lottie said, as if teasing me.

"No! Oh my goodness how awful." I shook my head. "He actually killed a lady?"

"No, curiously he did not kill her," Sebastian said, approaching the table with the newspaper.

"Who was this victim?" I asked. "And what did he do to her?" I was not sure I really wanted to know.

"It's someone we know! Listen to this," Lottie said, taking the newspaper back from Sebastian and barely containing the excitement in her voice. "London's infamous Madame Gwenfrida was attacked earlier this week by the Vigilante Slasher. The woman, who runs a house of disrepute in London's East End, described how he overpowered her. She was discovered by Inspector Stone of Scotland Yard, shackled to her bed with a cross scratched into her inner left arm and the Slasher had taken a lock of her hair as a trophy."

"So, the Vigilante Slasher still left his mark?" I said, knowing that he usually killed his victims leaving their left arm with a slash, rather than a scratch, as if marking his prey.

Sebastian pointed to the page. "But unlike his previous victims, he spared her life."

"And there's a picture and Madame Gwenfrida is..."

"Ah," I said. "Freddie Doyle."

"You knew?" Lottie said, her mouth agape.

"Purnell called her Madame when he was first introduced to her at Moor House. He must have known her alternative identity all along." I shook my head, wondering how the Duke of Loxborough would know of her. "What reason does the reporter give for the Slasher attacking Freddie?"

"They don't, really, but she mentions her wish for a new life and that the Slasher had convinced her to travel," Lottie said reading from the paper. "He said to her 'I don't kill women so leave town.' And Freddie's gushing about the man, saying he's given her a new perspective on life. But that's not all," Lottie said, wide-eyed as she turned the pages.

Sebastian laughed as the large newspaper sheets became caught up in Lottie's hands and he took it from her, finding the correct page. "There," he said passing it to me.

I read aloud from the page. "The British Museum have recovered the stolen sphinx amulet after it was handed in anonymously."

I sat down in the chair. "It clearly was not recovered by Inspector Stone. I'm sure he would have taken the credit if he had located it," I said.

"The Vigilante Slasher must have recovered it from Freddie and handed it in!" Lottie said, her eyes wide open.

My mouth felt dry. Only a few people in the world knew that Freddie Doyle was in possession of the amulet. But I pushed the thought from my mind. Freddie was clearly well known in London as her alias and the Slasher may have had her on his radar for some time, and then by coincidence discovered the amulet about her person. Or maybe following the incident Freddie handed it in herself anonymously? But a trickle of doubt lingered throughout the afternoon. One thought dominated my mind:

Have I been in the presence of the Vigilante Slasher?

* * *

Did you miss the characters from Branden Bay? John Breckon, Norma, Mrs Flint and Angus Hardy? If so, they will be making a reappearance!

Lady Ellen, finds herself entangled in a murder mystery when a renowned dance teacher is found dead in the ballroom of The Grand Hotel. The victim had no shortage of admirers and enemies alike.

As Ellen delves into the case, she uncovers a web of secrets and motives surrounding the enigmatic dance instructor. With the help of her trusted sidekicks she must navigate a treacherous dance of deception to unravel the truth. The stakes are raised when the police consider Mrs. Flint, the victim's last student of the day, the prime suspect.

Find out what happens in *A Body in the Ballroom*

Acknowledgments

I'd like to thank my creative writing tutor Rosemary Dun, both inside the OU and out! You encouraged me to pursue novel writing and gave me so much information and guidance, I'm still reading the handouts! You are amazing. Thanks also goes to my brilliant mentors Alison Knight and Jenny Kane of Imagine Creative Writing and their Novel in a Year course, which gave me lots of help and kept me on track and for continuing to be dear friends.

Thanks to the inspirational friends I met through the Romantic Novelists' Association, and the Bristol writing community (I'm too scared to list everyone in case I miss someone off!) And to my Beta readers, Tara Starling, Cinnomen Matthews McGuigan, and Michelle Armitage. Thanks also to Helen Blenkinsop who is a guru on the 'hook' and amazon ads. And thanks to my best writing friends – Callie Hill, Claire O'Conner and Jenny Treasure, for also being beta readers and for sharing the journey with me. And to my Cozy mastermind, especially Scarlett and my accountability partners Soraya, Halana and Kari. My

Editor Becky Halls who is more than an editor and also an inspiration. And not forgetting my mate Andy who makes life fun! And a huge thank you to Laura who really added a massive dose of inspiration for this particular book ;)

Thank you to my advance reader team who are really supportive and there for me, even from the first book.

Thank you to those on my mailing list who interact with me.

And thank you to Victoria Tait for helping me out so much when I needed it most.

Thank you to Tammy and all who look after Northmoor House and keep it preserved so that it can be an inspiration to the people who stay there.

Thanks to my family for supporting me, especially Gary for putting up with me tapping away at the keyboard 24/7.